the Rape *of the* Muse

ALSO BY MICHAEL STEIN

michael stein

the Rape *of the* Muse

THE PERMANENT PRESS
Sag Harbor, NY 11963

For information, address:
  The Permanent Press
  4170 Noyac Road
  Sag Harbor, NY 11963
  www.thepermanentpress.com

Library of Congress Cataloging-in-Publication Data

Stein, Michael–
    The rape of the muse / Michael Stein.
        p. cm.
    ISBN 978-1-57962-223-7 (hardcover : alk. paper)
        1. Artists—Fiction. 2. Male friendship—Fiction.
    3. Competition (Psychology)—Fiction. 4. Trials (Libel)—
    Fiction. 5. Trials (Slander)—Fiction. 6. New Haven
    (Conn.)—Fiction. I. Title.

PS3569.T3726R37 2011
813'.54—dc22   2011025845

Printed in the United States of America.

For Judy and Marty,

Protectors of the Muse

Don't let's forget the little emotions are the great captains of our lives, and that we obey them without knowing it.

—*Vincent van Gogh letter to Theo van Gogh, 1889*

CHAPTER 1

The first day of the trial, that clear, cool May morning ten years ago, I spotted Binny outside the Connecticut superior courthouse. I missed her pale freckled smile terribly, but I knew she wouldn't smile if she caught me spying. Even as I hid behind the solid columns of the judicial building's front entrance, I remembered the sensation I'd had, thinking how beautiful she was in the dusty light of the slide projector, every angle of her face flawless, the first night we'd met nine months before. But we'd spoken only once, briefly, after the infamous picture was published in January. She had called to tell me it was over between us. I was twenty-four and it nearly destroyed me.

The courthouse was six blocks away from the museum where Montrose and Pruhar had spent many hours talking about art together over the years. The columned front seemed far away from the university buildings farther down Chapel Street—cool, gray, gargoyled Gothic libraries and ivy-covered townhouses with wreaths on the door knockers and wrought-iron fences, now home to the Slavic and Philosophy departments—*and* from the commerce of downtown New Haven. The rear of the building emptied onto a concrete plaza and the businesses of Church Street, restaurants, law offices and canopied clothing stores with windows open to an unusually bright and sharply shadowed Wednesday.

I followed Binny into the marble front hall. The uniformed guards—from the paper bags on their table I could tell they were coffee and cruller addicts—directed me through a metal detector that was dwarfed by the glorious thirty-foot ceiling of the atrium. Globes of opaque glass splashed a mild light onto the gelled hair of the lawyers who hurried past carrying thick black leather bags. The cold stone floor discouraged children from running, and the silence made people look at their shoes as they squeaked across the fearsome white squares.

At the far end of the atrium outside a clerk's office was a bulletin board displaying the daily criminal calendar and a blood drive announcement. Under green marble arches, echoing corridors ran left and right toward the courtrooms. There were dark wooden benches along the walls where families, friends, wives, children, and lovers of plaintiffs and defendants waited. The smell of human confinement mixed with the odors of polished wood, wax, and dust.

Twenty steps ahead, I watched Binny enter Courtroom 11. When I got to the door, I saw the giant photographic portraits of the state's Supreme Court justices on the walls to either side, and a small wooden sign that read COURT IN SESSION. Courtroom 11, I'd read in the paper, had produced the indictments of pension thieves and police shooters, and recently of the mayor, named in a RICO case; his aides, represented by Boston attorneys, were already serving time. Connecticut had been settled in the seventeenth century by Puritan agitators who set about writing their own constitution, and the courts had rarely been empty since.

I was worried about how Montrose would perform at the trial. His lack of decorum was legendary. I'd seen him interrupt somber occasions before. As often as I'd seen him extend himself for young, unknown artists or act playful with his beloved cats, I'd also seen him grow loud in order to smash moments of silence and sentiment that made him uncomfortable. He spoke without inhibition; he said out loud what was on everyone's mind. I remembered his wife Cynthia saying to me after one of their arguments, "He wants me to agree with him all the time. He thinks that's love. I think it's babysitting." The thought of him sitting before a judge made me nervous, although I knew that as a born storyteller he would be a conduit for pure emotion about art for those of us who cared.

In the courtroom, wooden benches, identical to those in the hall, ran in rows toward a wooden fence beyond which sat the lawyers and their clients at two long tables. Beside the table on the right, the stenographer sat with her back to us, almost directly in front of the witness box. All courtrooms feel like closed tombs, the windows sealed and curtains pulled. I'd lost sight of Binny and the only splash of color I noticed was Molly Vidian, the reporter who had published the now famous *Vanity Fair* article and its possibly libelous picture in the January 2000 issue. In the front row, with a yellow pad on her lap, she sat equidistant from Montrose and the plaintiff, Simon Pruhar, and directly in front of Judge Miller who presided from a raised platform in a high-backed swivel chair. I could only see him from the chest up. In his vividly white shirt, the judge gave away nothing at either first or second glance. Directly over his head, the three grapevines and a ribbon insignia of Connecticut was cut into the wooden paneling. Montrose, staring at the judge, would at least appreciate the fine craftsmanship of his surroundings. On the judge's desk were a low lamp, a microphone, and a gold plastic water pitcher.

The courtroom was packed. The computer image that Montrose had published in the first *Vanity Fair* of the new millennium made plenty of people in the art world angry. The high-brow art magazines had lined up against him. He had made people furious for years (those who didn't love him), but *The Rape of the Muse* drew special attention. The art writers started in on Montrose almost immediately, weeks before Pruhar decided to sue, and I sometimes wondered if all the publicity, and the possibility of generating even greater publicity, was the reason Montrose's oldest friend had brought the case against him. Despite the long tradition of rape scenes in classical art, the critic at *ArtForum* called Montrose's picture "psychotically bizarre." One *Art in America* columnist wrote,

"For all his lasting work, whether Harris Montrose likes it or not, his identifying image may be a retributive Rape scene." The *Boston Globe* took a wry tone and saw the trial as a way to take a slap at both the art world and Connecticut. "The great tabloid narrative of 2000 is starting up in the Constitution state," began the story that topped their Sunday magazine. Usually, art interested a relatively small number of Americans—some academics, wealthy people with non-professional investors' interest, a handful of men and women in business and philanthropy, a certain subset of foundations and publishing houses, the dwindling few who read the art sections of big city newspapers—but the *Vanity Fair* picture, and now the trial, had interested a far wider audience.

Journalists with their narrow spiral notebooks crowded the courtroom, but I knew plenty of other faces. There were artists, and there were also people who barely knew Montrose, but wanted to come out in support. The carpenter who built pedestals for the sculptures that made Montrose famous in the 1970's was there; also one of the roofers who'd just finished work on Montrose's Abar Lake house, and the counter man from the bakery where Montrose bought his white cakes. Montrose bonded with them over cats, sports, desserts, any subject they wanted to discuss, and now they'd shown up for the opening arguments.

Friends of mine wondered what Montrose had been thinking when he agreed to publish *The Rape of the Muse*. The very artist who had disappeared to New Haven twenty-five years earlier had opened himself to cameras, gossip, and a lawsuit. I agreed it was no small matter, and I told my friends that he *wasn't* thinking. Yet I knew Montrose had made an image of exactly what *was* on his mind, a fantastic composition done without compromise or apology. The picture had ruined things between Binny and me.

Still, I think that he was surprised by the lawsuit. But if he was, he never showed it after the papers were served the second week in January, an unlucky thirteen days after *Vanity*

Fair hit the newsstands. As soon as he heard that he was being sued by Pruhar—a friend for thirty years, one of his greatest admirers—Montrose was ready to fight. He didn't mind litigation. Over the years he'd threatened to sue dealers who hadn't produced the catalogs they promised; he had fought neighbors over fence boundaries. There was nothing more entertaining to him than our legal system. Montrose followed every celebrity trial on CNBC or Court TV; he approved of Geraldo's gossip and ravings; he developed his own theories and countertheories of the latest cult group murder in California. Over the inheritance of their father's money, Montrose had been sued by his brother for a decade; he embraced the antagonism. He was litigious by nature, but usually *he* was the instigator, the aggressor.

At my last visit to the studio three weeks earlier—he didn't need me to do any framing or studio work as he prepared for the trial—he had reeled off other recent art-related legal cases. He had followed them over the years like he followed the O. J. and JonBenét Ramsey cases. Lichtenstein had been sued for using a diagram from a book on Cézanne, Warhol for modifying a photograph of a flower. Jeff Koons had settled out of court for creating a sculpture of puppies that looked remarkably like a picture produced by an amateur photographer.

When I phoned to ask Cynthia how he was on the eve of the trial, she said, "I don't know how to answer. He's insane about this. He goes on and on until I tell him I'll run away." Sitting at the defendant's table, Montrose looked dry-lipped and anxious. Who wanted to be charged with libel? But besides the possibility of a guilty verdict and a multimillion dollar settlement, what was at stake was the long view of all the work he had done over three decades: a lost court case would be the headline of his obituary.

At nine AM, Judge Miller spoke to the jury. "This case is an action by Mr. Pruhar to recover damages. In essence, his complaint states that the defendant, who is an artist, had printed in the magazine *Vanity Fair* a computer-generated picture. It is claimed that the picture *The Rape of the Muse* depicted or portrayed the plaintiff as a violent criminal, a portrayal which this plaintiff says is false.

"It is further claimed that when the defendant offered this computer image to *Vanity Fair*, he did so deliberately and with calculated intent to subject the plaintiff to hatred, contempt and ridicule, and that act caused him to be defamed.

"This is an action sounding in what we call defamation. Mr. Pruhar says that his reputation and professional standing have been diminished and he has been caused to suffer embarrassment, humiliation, mental pain, and anguish.

"There are two claims in consequence of what he says he suffered. He asks for $2 million in compensatory damages, in addition to which he asks for $5 million in what we call punitive damages, the kind of damages that are imposed in order to deter others from doing the same thing.

"Naturally, Mr. Montrose denies the allegation of the complaint, otherwise we wouldn't be here."

I heard the judge, but I was as preoccupied by Binny's whereabouts in the courtroom as I had been the night I'd met her the previous August at a lecture in New York.

It was my final night in the city before moving to New Haven, and my old professor, Miles Burr, had invited me to a talk featuring two women painters, one of whom was his old friend. The lecture was held in an NYU classroom that I knew well from my art school days, with its shiny concrete floor and mismatched chairs. I was glad to be out and about in Manhattan on a summer night, so I'd dressed formally for the talk in a black shirt with a black and white polka dot tie, black pants, and pointy boots.

With the shades drawn, the lecture room was half-dark at five PM. I stood in the back, every seat taken. The two painters drank diet Cokes and shared a slide projector mounted on a high stool. With the windows open, I could smell the fish market a block away. The fan on the projector forced the women to speak loudly, and every time someone moved, the metal-bottomed chairs sounded like matches striking the rough floor. I was listening to the talk half-heartedly, more intent on a woman with pearl earrings, jeans, and luminous skin, wearing black shoes as pointy as my own, sitting on the aisle seat three rows forward. She had bare ankles and the width of her Achilles tendon—the proportion of the Achilles tendon width to the calf, the way it left the heel and entered the calf, which was not easy to paint and made a woman's leg beautiful—was perfect. Small with spiky black hair, she was the only woman in the room wearing heels. She was working on a toothpick that she spun carefully between her index finger and thumb. Her sweater was sky blue.

The artists spoke in long sentences. One of them had a voice like a gerbil wheel. For the most part I believe artists should have their tongues cut out. To distract myself, I stared at the spinning toothpick, trying to make the blue sweater turn toward me.

When the talk was over, Burr palled with the one of the artists for a few minutes. He'd been her teacher too, years earlier. She had a willful chin and teeth like Eleanor Roosevelt. When he introduced me as Montrose's new assistant, she said, "He's a very funny man, I remember, but he lives on the outskirts of civilization. In New Haven, isn't it?" Burr couldn't get a nice word out of her. She thought that because Montrose hadn't shown his work in twenty-five years he was superfluous, pathetically out-of-step with the major art currents.

Antsy, I went over to the woman in blue who was standing alone. If she took off her shoes, I figured her at five foot two. I could tell that she liked wearing heels, and probably did whenever she could, even if they were hell on her feet.

"What'd you think?" I asked. When she looked at me, I looked away.

"As lethal as the recipe allows," she said.

"That bad?"

"Don't you think?"

15

I could tell she was fresh and rough, and I was grateful that she spoke to me at all.

At first, she didn't ask me about myself. She wasn't going to pretend that she cared. She knew her own strength and had things on her mind. She was looking me over and talking, testing, trying me out. Not unfriendly. But not exactly friendly either.

Soon enough, I admitted to Miss Elizabeth ("call me Binny") Sanford that I hadn't really been listening to the two painters either, that I was in town working for Harris Montrose, whom she'd never heard of. I told her that I'd watched golf on TV the other day (when I should have been working) and enjoyed it, which worried me. No twenty-four-year-old should enjoy golf. I told her that the tones on my television were off, the greens appeared as a terrible lime, so I'd gotten rid of the color and I'd never fully appreciated the pleasures of black and white before, even though I was a painter. I told her that I laughed at things if I could and I almost always found something funny about my life or my cat's. I told her I loved my truck and I didn't understand people who left dents unrepaired; I wanted to do their bodywork myself, paint it up.

She said that one of the guest artists was a friend of a friend, but that after hearing the talk she wasn't planning to introduce herself to the woman, that if she got rich she wanted to buy a townhouse in San Francisco, that she adored children, particularly her nephew Timmy, that she had a roommate who had just moved to Baltimore, but still paid half the rent, and the only thing she missed about her was how well she did the laundry. Then she said, "Oh, and you shouldn't stare."

For the first time she looked at me directly as if to say, Get Ready. I could smell her then: ginger.

"No, I shouldn't," I said.

"You live in the city?"

"Starting tomorrow, New Haven, Connecticut," I said.

"What part of that beautiful city?"

"Downtown."

"Near Toad's Place?"

"Two blocks away. How do you know Toad's?" Toad's was a club on York Street, not far from the New Haven Coliseum.

"I saw a show there. A girl band. Your basic ambient drone, the sounds of self-pity."

"You drove up for the show?"

"That's what I do. I write about music."

She looked me over, skipping my eyes.

"Shitty little place," she said. "But I have a warm spot for it."

"It's not so bad. Good donuts."

"So you didn't like the talk?" she finally asked me, smiling.

All I knew was that her smile meant a lot of things at once. I grinned back, but I felt I was making a fool of myself. She was playing with me and I wasn't used to it.

"I guess I'm not a still-life kind of guy," I said.

"Who taught you to talk like that?"

Did I love her right then? Of course I did.

Burr had called me the next morning to ask where I'd gone after his friend's talk. "Beautiful girl," he said when I told him. He'd noticed her. "The total spice rack."

Eight months later, in the courtroom—I finally spotted Binny in the second row near the front on the left—if she spoke to me at all I wasn't sure what I would say.

When Montrose finally met her, he had noticed her too. He'd made her the Muse.

CHAPTER 2

I had no intention of leaving New York the morning I took Interstate 95 north into Connecticut, but I was happy to get out of town on a steamy July day and curious to meet Harris Montrose, if only to bring a few juicy details back to the city. The word in the art world of 1999 was that Montrose, having blown his career long ago, now lived in sad seclusion. The story of Montrose was a tireless, looming presence among my art school gang. Although he was seldom discussed in artistic terms, he was analyzed as mystical, political, apocalyptic. After his famous 1972 sculpture exhibition, Montrose had a lineup of enthusiasts, collectors, curators, and reputation caretakers ready to go to work for him and make him a phenomenon. But then he disappeared. Suddenly gone from public view, he had supposedly cloistered himself in New Haven and lost his taste and nerve for big-time action. Montrose passed into myth. His work had made it into books and the slide talks of every figure drawing class in America for a brief while, and then he simply vanished.

I had pestered Burr, an old friend of Montrose's, for half a year before he arranged my visit to New Haven. Burr knew that I'd recently lost my Brooklyn girlfriend and along with her my ability to paint. I hadn't done anything new in months; I looked at my empty canvases as though they'd snuck into my studio in the middle of the night. I couldn't look at any of my friends' work because it reminded me of what I wasn't doing, couldn't do. A visit to Montrose would jolt me into action. Why had he dropped out? I wanted fame badly and he'd given it up.

I drove all the way with my windows open, enjoying the sunshine and in a good mood. The rump of my red pickup was pushed by eighteen-wheelers driving grocery store pastries toward Boston. The insurance cities of Connecticut were the airless glass modules I remembered. Southern Connecticut smelled of pine trees and ocean, but the landscape just outside New Haven was a wasteland: small industry, mobile home parks, shopping centers with McDonalds and Home Depots. The first billboard in the city was for a strip club, "serving lunch."

The highway curled around the city and lowered me onto narrow streets with nineteenth-century houses. I followed the directions Montrose's wife had faxed me, going away from the university toward the leafier northern edge of town with its blue mailboxes and wet slate drying in lacy patterns. Despite a withering summer, New Haven was still blooming green and yellow and smelled like roses. Coming from Manhattan, it was country to me. The houses were big, the driveways were big, the hydrangea were so full they blocked windows. Gardeners' trucks with their grassy, open-caged trailers littered with mowers and rakes and blue tarpaulins, were parked on every other block.

Montrose's house was beside a small lake (bodies of water always seemed improbable in cities), hidden behind a head-high evergreen wall. Shingled, three stories tall with a cupola, its beautiful Victorian trimmings had been confidently updated and recently repainted. As I turned into the driveway, I noticed four of Montrose's sculptures perched on the low-pitched roof over the front door. His studio was in a carriage house attached to the main house by a glass walkway. Already I knew I wanted to live like this someday: space, serenity, privacy. There was a giant sculpture of a walking tree—*Green Man*, it was called—set in a patch of forest, ferns and pines, at the top of the circular drive, directly in front of the studio. A heroic figure, if there ever was one. I had seen pictures of the *Green Man*; they hadn't done justice to his height, now that I stopped to really look. He stood under a thirty-foot-high glass gazebo, shaded from the rain. Or rather he strode, his trunk-legs set apart, contrapposto. Looking up, I saw blue sky through the roof.

The studio door had a wind chime instead of a buzzer. When he saw me through the glass, Montrose signaled for me to come in. An alarm sounded, far off in the house, until I closed the door behind me.

"You have my coffee?"

I shook my head. Was I supposed to have brought coffee? If he was teasing me, I couldn't tell.

Montrose wore a stained blue T-shirt which he hadn't tucked into khaki shorts. His shoulders curled forward, heavily muscled. Brown eyes were set in deep sockets. His shaving technique had left patches of gray whisker under his jawline. Montrose sat at an unfinished wooden table that looked as if it had been built the week before. On it were several small hand drills and circular containers of bits, a can of paste wax, and a line of empty paper coffee cups. He picked up a small piece of bronze flash and began to burnish it with hand tools. His fingers were strangely delicate. He put on a headpiece like a miner's, and flipped down magnifying lenses in front of his eyes. He flicked on the motor near his forearm. It hummed softly. At the far end of the surface was a computer monitor.

"You don't mind if I work while we talk, do you?" he asked, and turned down the radio. His head was huge, his hair uncombed, uncut, graying. He talked with his hands, which jutted and poked. When he crossed his legs, I saw he was wearing black sneakers and no socks. In an old photograph I'd seen in Professor Burr's office at school, Montrose was hunched over a chessboard in the same posture he took in front of me. Even in the 1970's his hair was a mess, and he had the same dark, intense expression, his big arm pushing a pawn forward. He was jowlier in his mid-fifties.

"Why didn't you take the teaching job in Burr's department? You're looking at an art career aren't you?" he asked over the low whir of his machine.

He sipped from a Dunkin' Donuts cup; he already had coffee. His first question to me about bringing coffee seemed forward, but intimate in a way.

"Yes, I am," I said. *Looking* at an art career? Before my recent dry spell in the studio, my paintings had been well-received. I had been picked the year before by the *New York Times* as one of "25 painters under 25." Had Burr told Montrose that he'd offered me an instructorship, but mentioned nothing about my success?

"You know, people don't buy much art," Montrose said, "unless they're redoing a living room or an office building."

"Aren't people always redoing their living rooms?" I asked.

"Not many. Not often enough."

Montrose's studio was divided into three parts and lit by forty-foot skylights. Silver half tones came into the far end of the studio through large windows, and at this noon hour there was a watery essence to the space. It smelled of dust and burnt oil. I scanned the room, spying for new work I'd be able to describe to friends when I got home. At our end of the space, there was a closeness, where the ceiling fell abruptly from forty feet to ten. We sat near to the front window, looking out past the *Green Man* in his forest glen, down the sloping front lawn, over the hedges, and across the street at Abar Lake.

I didn't have to tell Harris Montrose why I hadn't taken the university job. I didn't have to tell a man like him that a working artist couldn't thrive in an environment of academic small-mindedness. I considered Burr's offer to teach alongside him and I turned it down the same day, knowing I'd probably get myself fired for insubordination after a while anyway and be out on the street.

"I know your name is Rand, but what's your real name?" Montrose asked sympathetically, as if it had disfigured me.

"Rand," I told him.

"Are you sure?" His tone was one of disbelief. For years I had turned away from calls for Randall and Randolph. I usually told people my name was short for Random. My father had named me after a Rand McNally atlas. When I complained that no one got my name right, not even my teachers, my father told me I was lucky I hadn't been called kilometer or F-4, the spot on the grid where he found our hometown in the state of Massachusetts. "Builds character," he said. Despite this geographical history, I barely got off my block before I was fourteen. The few trips I took were on buses with my grandmother to visit my grandfather and his failing kidneys in the hospital. His bed stank of piss and I couldn't keep my eyes off the bag of urine hanging from the bed rail.

"You're a tall one, Rand. Aren't you too tall to be an artist? Burr says you're good with your hands. He says you have an eye and don't mind hard work. He says you know computers."

"I know a bit," I said.

"That's what I need help with. I've been doing these prints," he said. He leaned over and patted his orange machine. "Computer images. Cyberspace," he sniggered and pointed toward the wall at the far end where some prints hung.

"I've heard of it," I told him.

"Easier work than sculpting. Cleaner too. No messy doorknobs."

At NYU, there were rumors that Montrose had gone crazy. If he worked at all it was assumed he was an aging hack. In art school, we'd played the game of killing off the current crop of art heroes and coming up with instant obituaries. My pals would be unhappy to hear that Montrose still made art. It was easier to picture Montrose in a fugue state in the suburbs, glowering at the Bible or TV.

"Let's take a walk inside," he said. "I need more coffee. You want one?"

"I don't do coffee," I told him.

He looked at me suspiciously. "Never?"

"Three times a year. Special occasions."

"Well, next time you should still bring one for me anyway. It's the polite thing to do you know. I'm a fiddler and a diddler," he said, rising from his hunched position. "I'm a realist. Sure I hope that people will see that I invented a new kind of figure, what Rodin and Giacometti did. My wife says I'm always getting myself in trouble for what I say to people. But I only tell the truth. You can't get in trouble for that."

Montrose walked out of the studio through a narrow glass corridor filled with sculptures, carved horns, and tiny rocks that looked like mountains.

"Where's *your* studio?" he asked when we reached the kitchen. Over the cabinets was a row of Eskimo war clubs. A lithograph of Burr's hung above the sink. The coffeemaker sat near a dish of pill bottles—Advil, calcium, multivitamins, packets of Nicorettes, a box of toothpicks. He poured the last two inches into his Dunkin' Donuts styrofoam cup and put it in the dark cave of the microwave.

"Avenue B." I was living in unfinished space above a grocery store run by an angry gay man who was also my landlord. He had recently screamed at me for ten minutes near the cold case because I'd misplaced my key.

Montrose almost smiled, as if a memory were passing through him. "Low rent."

"Not as low as you'd think."

"What do you need a car for?" he asked, gesturing at my red pickup parked out front.

"I like the feeling that I can get away when I have to. Nineteen-ninety model that I fixed up."

"You fix cars too, huh."

"It's how I got into paint," I said. "My uncle owned a garage. He let me spray all the bodywork."

"What do your parents think of your career?"

I reported that my father was not happy but that he wasn't really paying attention; all day in his accounting firm, all evening in the den where he kept his nautical supplies, his treasured

23

antique compasses, the underwater topologic maps, the anchors, photos of lighthouses, and harpoon lamps. My mother just wanted to know if I was making a living. The truth was that I owed more money than I had. Since graduating art school, I'd been working part-time in the basement of the Metropolitan Museum for the Asian Art Conservation Department, mixing patinas and glazes; and at night and very early in the morning painting in my studio—or more recently, failing to paint.

Outside, walkers hustling around Abar Lake in exercise gear peeked between the evergreens. Those who weren't completely tuned into their Walkmen saw Montrose's thirty-foot tree-man in his magical garden at the end of the driveway, a tree without limbs or leaves, with holes where shoulders should have been, with a lumpy, barky surface. They looked again, unsure, and then strolled up the driveway as if they'd been invited, as if this were a museum. They stopped at his feet and stared up. Montrose seemed used to seeing them out his window and shrugged.

It was the Bible stories he'd sculpted—the Four Horsemen of the Apocalypse, the Casting Out of Satan—that had pushed Montrose into the mythic realm in 1972. Because these sculptures were about cataclysm but also about goodness, the Republican representative from Louisiana—a friend of Montrose's parents in New Orleans—discussed them on the floor of Congress, making them instantaneously of interest to the whole world. These sculptures were a comment on the war in Vietnam, the congressman announced. Wasn't it the Bible that separated Americans from the Vietnamese we were fighting five thousand miles away that year? Bible stories were at the core of our culture, the lessons terrifying and primal. Congressman Lindell never had to mention that Montrose had sculpted naked figures. At the same time, this nakedness excited the young artists, Burr's students and thousands of others, who were looking for a new potency in art that in those days was famously abstract. These were the figures

24

Montrose became known for, twisted, off-balance, creating a new sculptural space for old stories. Figures snaked, turned toward each other, entwined, wore wings. They sat astride each other, splayed, touched wildly. Of course Montrose did not approve of debauchery, his conservative defenders noted. He'd sculpted tales of fury and doom, of excess; bodies fell toward hell; it spoke of our future if the war in Southeast Asia wasn't won. His art seemed to say something wonderful about American vigor and fearlessness when America needed to hear it. There was a hunger for something to endure at a time when the world was out of control, and Montrose's life-sized sculptures seemed permanent, Burr explained.

He was the opposite of the last art hero, the mysterious Jackson Pollock, whose painting twenty years earlier, at the start of the Cold War, also represented freedom. Pollock asserted nothing, asked nothing, warded off inquiries, gave no advice, just smoked and stared. Montrose was publicly aggressive. He attacked his fellow artists and their non-figurative art. Wasn't this ferociousness another quality to show the Vietnamese? Montrose was suddenly a hero everyone could root for. For a full year he was the biggest news there was in the art world. The hungry press was eager to see him. But as soon as he was famous, he began to withdraw, to hide from all the people who wanted to shake his hand. He didn't want to be photographed with the congressman who invited him to Washington.

As we walked back to the studio, I started to tell him about my painting, but he made it clear that he didn't want to *hear* about my pictures. Some day, he said, he wanted to see them. At his desk, he put down his coffee and flipped on his computer. I was unprepared for the beauty of the images that appeared. In New York that year, computer prints hadn't generated much interest. My art school classmates were using computers as drawing tools, or to morph and play with advertising logos; or they made the computer the subject of their art by running hokey video games. The Great Art of the twentieth century, Abstraction, had already been done—that was the standard thinking—and it certainly didn't include cyber images. Montrose was a sculptor; what was he doing trying to work on a computer? I suppose I should have looked for weakness in his new work as my friends would have, but I loved the pictures immediately. I tried to memorize every inch of them.

Behind me, I heard the door open. "You bring me one of those?" Montrose asked the small, elegant man who came into the studio just then and pointed at his supersized coffee.

"Rand, this is Simon Pruhar."

"We've been introduced, haven't we?" Pruhar asked.

I was surprised and delighted that he remembered me. Burr had told me that Pruhar, Montrose's oldest friend and New Haven neighbor, often visited the studio. I'd met Pruhar four years before when Burr had invited him to speak to our class about welding. I recalled that Pruhar's art was less impressive than he was. He wasn't dark or dramatic or pained or contemptuous. Hands plunged into his pockets, he moved slowly when he spoke to us, explaining styles and the reasons for his tastes. When challenged, he seemed unguarded. He laughed easily. His innocence played well with most of the women.

"It really is true that you know everyone," Montrose said to Pruhar, shaking his head. "You get around."

"You've usually had your coffee by now," Pruhar said. His corduroys were pressed, his shirt purple linen. He had beautiful teeth, a perfect smile, and a thin ridgeless nose.

"That doesn't mean I don't want another one. Now listen. I'm having a show in New York in October," Montrose said casually.

Had I heard him correctly? I had always prided myself on ignoring the fame of the famous—I never stared at celebrities I passed on the streets of New York—but calming myself at that moment would have required exceptional measures. The muscles in my cheeks began to twitch; my throat was suddenly parched. Was Montrose really planning a comeback? A New York show? I understood that a public hungry for the newest movie didn't pay attention to sculpture or painting or computer images, but his return would shake the art world.

"You're what?" Pruhar asked. He was as stunned as I was. He tugged at his right ear, tipping his head that way, his thick hair bouncing. He ignored the cat rubbing against his leg.

"The computer pieces."

"Naturally, what else," Pruhar said, trying to stay cool. "There's nothing like them out there. You'll be avant-garde."

"Well, there it is. I haven't had a show in twenty-five years."

"It's time," Pruhar said.

If I went twelve months without a show, friends would pound on my studio door shouting, "Police. Homicide. Is someone dead in there?" One year was too long without a review if you wanted to reach the big time. Montrose had been gone for nearly three decades, known to those of us who'd been through art school as the most original artist of the last generation, but also as a cautionary tale. He'd disappeared without a goodbye exhibition, without any farewell gesture, without signs of surrender or tough talk, without bitterness.

"Don't you think it's time, Rand?" Pruhar asked, trying to bring me into the conversation.

I was thrilled but didn't want to fawn, which I sensed wouldn't go over well with Montrose. I wanted to convince him of my pure, incorruptible spirit—who needed a show? But I didn't believe this, nor did Pruhar who was eager for me to agree without hesitation. I felt if I said the wrong thing, made one wrong move, I would lose something I didn't even know I'd wanted when I arrived: Montrose's validation.

I was suddenly bashful, and Pruhar moved on. "You have a gallery?" he asked.

"Yes I do," Montrose said. Even as I listened I found the temperature of my skin rising with excitement.

"You didn't tell me you were even looking," Pruhar said, offended.

"I wasn't."

It was my lucky day. One hour in Connecticut and I was one of two artists in the world who knew Montrose's plans. I was acting as if this was no big deal. But of course it was *huge* news.

Pruhar, still a little startled himself, asked, "Which gallery?"

"Nora Cengal," Montrose said.

"Never heard of her."

"Beauty is making a comeback," Montrose said idly. "If artists set out to make something beautiful instead of trying merely to be original, we'd be better off.

"I keep asking Simon the difference between beautiful and pretty, but he doesn't have an answer for me," Montrose said. I knew *he* had an answer, and this new work was it. I knew I was in the presence of great art when I looked away from a painting and couldn't recapture the experience unless I looked back; memory was inadequate. That was the spell cast by my first glance at his computer screen. He had scanned photos of trees and vines into the computer and placed them in landscapes where they'd never grown, shaping them into the silhouettes of human figures. The powerful curve of a woman's right hip had become Nature.

"Pruhar makes ceramics. He's into pretty now," Montrose said, turning to me. *Pretty* sounded like a curse, a snub; I felt the implied dishonor of it.

"So you're having a show," Pruhar repeated cautiously, calculating the logistics. "She's putting it together pretty fast, isn't she? Only three months lead time?"

"She said she would be ready for me in October," Montrose explained. "She was very sweet, really. She said people have been waiting for me. Why make them wait any longer?"

I knew Nora Cengal must have rearranged her entire season's schedule to accommodate Montrose. There were now artists in New York angry for having been bumped by a ghost from New Haven.

"Comebacks are very American, you know. This is fabulous. Fabulous. It makes me want to get a place to show in New York, too." Pruhar was slowly becoming excited.

"You haven't worked in months," Montrose pointed out.

"Not true, I've done those glazed plates."

"That's not work."

"I need to find a gallery to show my ceramics is all."

"Ceramics is not art," Montrose said dismissively. "You should be looking for a store, not a gallery. Bloomingdale's. Filene's."

"It's art to me," Pruhar said.

"Well it shouldn't be. You know better. You need to stop calling it art. You need to stop carrying around dishes and vases in suitcases trying to make people believe that it's serious work."

Pruhar ignored him. "Let me recall what you said twenty-seven years ago after your last show. You said, 'You either play this game or you don't. If you don't choose which, there'll always be trouble.'"

"I said that?" Montrose asked.

"Yes, you did."

"Well then I was right."

"So are you playing this game now? Again, finally, after twenty-five years?"

"Have you noticed how undisciplined my cats are?" Montrose answered, ducking Pruhar's question.

The two of them, Scout and Jake, had leapt onto the work table and stood on either side of the computer like guards. Montrose's desk was a mess—brushes, batteries, a Gesswein catalog of abrasives and metalwork tools, sucking candies, rubber bands, steel wool, sandpaper, paste wax, wood finish, rags, awls. The desk itself was balanced on oversized, upside-down orange parking cones glued to the floor. The floor was piled with extension cord, tapes, displays of snap-on rotary discs. For someone who didn't sculpt much anymore, Montrose spent a lot of time with his old supplies.

"Tell me why she won't take this piece for the show," Montrose asked, clicking a new image onto the screen.

"You've already discussed pieces?" Pruhar asked.

29

Montrose answered his own question. "I know why, really. She thinks it contains an irrelevancy."

"It's actually quite lovely," Pruhar said, looking over Montrose's shoulder. I stood just to Pruhar's left.

"Is it pretty or beautiful?"

"I don't know. Don't ask me that," Pruhar snapped.

"She says she can't sell it," he told Pruhar. "That's all she cares about."

"She's probably under forty. She'll learn," Pruhar said.

Montrose scrolled over the picture, magnified it, shrank it. Adobe Photoshop was the only computer program he had ever used, he told me, the only one he ever wanted to use. Montrose talked to me as if he'd known me for years, as if I were his equal. I was flattered, excitedly pleased. All this talk made me eager—eager to get back to New York and let on that Montrose was coming to town, eager to mimic his wonderful, comical, brutal monologue for friends, eager to paint a beautiful new piece and return to New Haven with it.

"These computers have something special," Montrose said. "If I use technology to help me with my figures, no one can accuse me of being retro. People are afraid to criticize computers."

"I remember when you were retro. You remember where you were living twenty-seven years ago?" Pruhar asked.

"Of course I do."

"Where was that?" I asked. My duty as Montrose's fan was to hear as much about him as I could.

"The Hotel Continental," Pruhar said. "Downtown, next to the YMCA."

"Downtown here?" I asked. I was still trying to pretend that nothing shocking had happened in the last ten minutes with the announcement of his show.

"Near Ninth Square. It was a derelicts' hotel. You rented the room by the day."

"By the week," Montrose corrected.

"There was a bathroom at the end of the hall, green walls, twenty-watt bulbs." Pruhar was smiling.

"It was down the block from the studio space we shared. And there was this greasy coffee shop on the ground floor of the hotel."

"I had bacon and eggs every morning. Boy, that was good. Now my wife won't let me have them," Montrose said, shaking his head. "I've come a long way. But I'm not sure it's gotten any better for me." He leaned his chair back and studied his latest image, but Scout blocked half the screen.

"Part of his mystique was living in that hotel," Pruhar told me with a sweet enthusiasm.

"It wasn't so bad," Montrose said.

"Why *did* you live there?" Pruhar asked, as though he'd been meaning to put this question to Montrose for years.

"I didn't have to clean up."

"I remember coming up one day to wake you at about one in the afternoon. We were on different schedules," Pruhar said. "I worked during the day, he worked all night. There were these cops in the hall when I got upstairs. I asked what had happened and they told me a man had been murdered in the next room. My first thought was: Harris killed him."

"Now come on," Montrose said. "You're scaring Rand."

"That was what I thought. You threatened people," Pruhar said.

"I didn't mean to."

"Physically."

"I never killed anyone."

"You were asleep and missed the whole thing."

"Who murdered him?" Montrose asked.

"I don't know. But you moved out a week later."

"Bad luck to have someone killed next door."

Montrose took a Nicorette out of his mouth and laid it on the workbench on its cellophane wrapper. From a bottle next to the computer he shook out a pale green pill.

"I hate this vitamin my wife gives me," he said to me in a low voice. "I resent its presence in my life. When you see her, I want you to tell her it's idiotic that I have to take this vitamin."

31

His wife came into the studio just then, as if she knew he had reached for his vitamin bottle.

"Rand thinks it's stupid that I have to take this vitamin. There's no evidence it helps, he says."

She looked at me and knew instantly I'd said nothing of the sort. "I'm Cynthia Montrose," she said, shaking my hand. Hers was soft and cool and felt recently lotioned. She looked back at her husband. "Just take it." She was small and brown-haired. Her wedding band was white gold, hammered thin, identical to his.

"You tell her, Rand," he said. "Tell her what I told you."

"It's not too much to ask," Cynthia interrupted. Her tone was both pleading and annoyed, as if they had been through this a thousand times before.

"It's a symbol, and you can't thrust your symbols at people."

"Why not?" she demanded.

"That's tyranny."

"Okay," she said, accepting his definition. "I'm okay with that."

He swallowed the pill without water.

"What were you visiting us for?" he asked as she turned to leave.

"You've already taken care of it." I could tell from the weary look in her eyes that she was used to his contrariness. She said appreciatively, "Oh, and I love the Chinese brush pot you left for me."

"It's for your pencils," he said.

"It's beautiful. Thank you."

When Cynthia left the room, he said, "She doesn't give up."

Of course his comeback would cause quite a stir. Could he survive the force of his re-emergence? Putting his work on display in New York might identify him as just another has-been. Perhaps the art world had lost interest in his work after twenty-five years away. He was as good as dead to most of the

New York art world. Of course the dead got special treatment in art; museums got interested in you when you were dead.

"I'll need help with frames for these pictures, and I'll want you to set the show up in New York," he said to me.

I looked over at Pruhar to see if Montrose was teasing. Had he really just offered me a job?

"It's what I'll be paying you for." Montrose turned to Pruhar. "He'll help them at the gallery like he'll help me here. He's a good boy."

I hadn't come to New Haven looking for work. I'd come to check out why Harris Montrose had abandoned Olympus and to see if he had done any new work in three decades. I was knocked off balance. At that moment, I thought quite unexpectedly, loudly inside my head: He is a great artist, and his greatness will make me great. This was what I'd been hoping for without knowing it. I would be able to paint again and my painting would be better than ever.

"Who have you told about this show?" Pruhar wanted to know.

"Who should I tell?"

"Your gallery will take care of getting the word out in the art press. Are they putting money behind this?"

"If people aren't interested, I'm not sure all the money in the world will get it done."

"Have you told Burr? If he gets his students there, they'll pass along the news."

"I should tell Burr." Montrose seemed unconcerned.

"This is very big," Pruhar said, getting excited all over again.

"It's not so big." Montrose tried to smile, shrugged instead. He refused to be optimistic. I could tell it made him uncomfortable.

"This will be *the* big show of the year. These prints will introduce the art of the new millennium," Pruhar said.

"Taking the side of Beauty always means a fight. But maybe these battles can be revisited every twenty-five years," Montrose said hopefully.

33

Who should I tell? The back of my neck was wet when I nervously touched it. I was ready to leave. The last hour had exhausted me.

When I was at the door Montrose called out, "We'll have time to talk about your hair next time?"

"My hair?"

"What did you do to it?" he asked. I had recently cut it very short. "Come on. You have to accept responsibility for it."

I was still unsure if he was teasing or if he was testing me in some way.

"You'll move up here and start work in a week or so?"

Without hesitation I said yes.

CHAPTER 3

After Judge Miller's introductory statement to the jury—
five men and three women who sat in faded red, folding
movie-theater seats—Pruhar was called to the stand. Dressed
in a beige suit and purple tie, Pruhar sat comfortably in the
witness box. His lawyer, a Mr. Barrow, led him through historical material about his training, his arrival in New Haven,
and where he'd taught. Barrow established Pruhar's credentials,
listed his one-man shows and awards, announced a resume
that seemed impressively endless. In the witness chair, Pruhar
appeared to be listening closely. Women had always found him
enormously charming and flooded him with sexual opportunities, according to Burr. He took none of them—worried over
dark conclusions—although his flirting skills were highly developed. From the rear left corner of the room, I looked over at
Rita Pruhar in the first row. I wondered how she was faring.
Her makeup was thick and perfect, but she seemed tired, slack.
She'd always had a soft spot for Montrose, who used to bum
cigarettes from her. She smoked to lose weight, but she looked
heavy now, sitting behind her husband's legal team. I also had a
good angle to watch Montrose. To see Montrose in a tie made
the whole business seem ridiculous.

Barrow stood at a lectern. His leading questions made
Pruhar come off as an educated man, a superior person.

"How long have you known Mr. Montrose?"

"Since 1970." I had to strain to understand Pruhar, who was speaking softly to give the impression of being in pain.

"That would be thirty years?"

"Yes. We met when I was in art school in New Orleans."

"And you were friends?"

"Close friends I would say." With me, Montrose resisted open talk of how close they were or what had brought them together thirty years earlier. "He was twenty, clean, hetero, and pretty mentally healthy," Montrose told me to put an end to it. "That was quite a lot for a person in New Orleans in those days."

Montrose told me that as a young man, Pruhar was fabulously handsome; in a world of gay dealers and curators ("Athenians," Montrose called them), he had played off his looks. "They quivered when they saw him," Montrose said. "They would do anything to help him. Married men are highly prized you know." Pruhar had a great charm and sure instincts. He was still familiar with every young artist who was hot; he read four art magazines a week.

Montrose had moved to Connecticut because Pruhar had taken a teaching job at the art school there. Pruhar, a student at Tulane, met Montrose hanging around the city of his birth, playing chess and sculpting, an art prodigy and a high school drop-out who loitered by the university soda machines. Pruhar and he had been arguing about art ever since; and when Pruhar and his wife fled the South, Montrose followed, taking the room in the Hotel Continental I'd heard about on my first visit to Abar Lake nine months earlier. More than once I'd overheard Montrose brag on the phone about Pruhar to curators or young artists who called for an opinion or some advice. Montrose thought his friend was a rarity, an artist with "a good eye," an abstract sculptor (Pruhar had bent and painted steel I-beams, mixed glass with charred stone in ungainly, tapering spinal columns) who could still appreciate a finely drawn figure. Montrose told me that in art school Pruhar used to keep all his sketches in case he became famous. But when he was twenty-four years old, Pruhar hedged his bets: he took the university job at Yale, created fewer pieces of his own, and saved his pennies. Pruhar had grown up poor, and in the studio they shared when they first arrived in New Haven, Pruhar used mousetraps twice, Montrose told me. Later, Pruhar developed expensive tastes; his spending was conspicuous. He wore cashmere socks. His energy, his schemes, engaged Montrose. He tried to make money on African antiques, on Eskimo art, on furniture from the Far East. He always lost large sums and then recovered somewhat, with great effort and Montrose's prodding. But Pruhar loved art deeply and Montrose loved him for that.

From the witness box, Pruhar's crossed legs poked out. He was wearing the beige cashmere socks Montrose had given him for Christmas. Was this an odd coincidence or a poke in Montrose's eye?

"Prior to January 2000 you saw him regularly?"

"Yes. I visited his studio on Abar Lake several times a week."

"You spoke to him often?"

"Nearly every day."

"You were more than professional acquaintances, weren't you? You traveled on vacations with him and his wife?"

"We did."

"Do you recall giving a sweet sixteen party for his daughter?"

"Yes."

"You gave this with your wife at your home?"

"Yes."

Montrose's lawyer—*Vanity Fair's* lawyer—Steven Pontes stood. Only when someone moved suddenly did I realize how motionless the courtroom was. The still-life aspect facilitated the drawings of judge and witnesses one saw on the evening news. As far as I knew, there hadn't been a meaningful show of court scene cartoons since Daumier. "Your Honor, I'm going to object to this line of inquiry. It seems highly irrelevant to me. This is ten years before the claimed incident and it relates to a sweet sixteen party."

After thirty years, Montrose and Pruhar knew everything about one another, told each other the details of their lives. When Montrose heard a story about someone important to Pruhar, he remembered it. He remembered the name of Pruhar's son's girlfriend who was a British bond trader, he remembered Pruhar's street address in New Orleans. When he first heard about the suit, Montrose told me, "Simon likes attention. And when he moans, he gets it, although not from his wife, she won't baby him."

"When did the difference grow up between the two of you regarding your aesthetic judgments, that is, as to your feeling about sculpture and styles?" Barrow asked Pruhar.

"Well, we always had a certain amount of difference about sculpture." Pruhar's sweetness made the question seem petty.

"Did you have ill will between you about that?"

"Not that ever affected our friendship."

"Did there come a time when the differences between your views, your respective views on art, when those differences were expressed bitterly or acrimoniously?"

"Yes, I would say that after I had some success in ceramics, after my work attracted some attention. He believed my view of art had changed. I was still sculpting and he didn't believe that I could sculpt *and* do stoneware.

"And he would be very acrimonious about that, he resented it." When he spoke, he often turned to the judge who not infrequently sipped from his black plastic mug. Judge Miller's robes made me think of Schuyler, how several of his landlords and the IRS would really have liked to have a word with him in a place like this.

And then, as if I were able to make him appear just by thinking of him, I spotted Schuyler across the courtroom. Why was Schuyler at the trial? I wondered if he'd surfaced just to see Montrose squirm.

I hadn't heard from him since Christmas, and his old girlfriend Melanie had called me in mid-April—when she'd seen news of the case about the picture in *Vanity Fair*—to tell me that Schuyler, my closest friend from art school, had disappeared again.

"He's been extremely depressed," she said. "He misses talking to you. He doesn't really have any friends except you."

I told Melanie that I would be of no help in finding him, but the thought of Schuyler depressed and alone made me terribly sad.

"I've spent too many nights not knowing where he is, who he's with, if he's dead or alive," Melanie said, sighing. "Half the time I'm in a rage wishing him dead, the other half I want to kill him myself. Meanwhile, I'm in torment waiting for the ambulance men or police to come to the door with bad news."

"There's no bad news. He'll be back. He loves you," I told her. Schuyler was usually low on cash and he was afraid to sleep alone, so he crashed where he could until he found another woman who couldn't live without him. When it ended, he returned to Melanie whom he relied on to take care of him, buy him cigarettes, and make him big breakfasts of fried eggs and pancakes, the one meal he ate each day.

When I was in despair, when the need for advice came over me, the first person I called was Schuyler. He'd been the first person I'd told about meeting Binny.

"So she's an arsonist," he'd said.

"A what?"

"An arsonist of the heart."

"I'm not denying it," I told him.

Schuyler was worried I'd lost my mind when I first told him that I was going to work for Montrose. He was concerned I would disappear by moving to the sticks, stop looking for a new gallery, stop trying to get into new shows. He assumed about me what I would have assumed about anyone who left: he's been beaten by the city. Why else would you leave Manhattan? When you're in your twenties in New York, you weren't supposed to care if what you saw or where you lived was beautiful. You were in New York for feeling and for truth, for drama, to be part of the greed and ecstasy and news. The whole city was magical from Hester Street up to Dyckman. I was drawn to it when I applied to art school. And once I was there, I resisted being shrunk to insignificance with all my might. I worked to be worthy and modesty never stood in the way.

But what I hadn't told him was that in the three months before moving to New Haven, I'd produced nothing. When I painted, I came up empty. My resolve to work had fallen apart. I looked for things that were easier to do than painting and made hours pass instead of the long minutes with a brush. When I forced myself to try again I got nowhere. It became harder to believe that discipline had anything to do with it. My smallest effort had become Trying Like Hell. I told myself not to panic, but this only induced panic, and the idea of never working again seemed normal. I blamed Pam; I'd broken up with her thinking it might help. When Schuyler called my studio, I yelled, "I'm painting," and hung up because I wasn't. I had always prided myself on the productivity of my hours alone, but I had changed from a long-haul truck to an idling bus.

He predicted I'd want out of New Haven in under two weeks. But he was wrong. I'd quickly fallen into a routine. Mondays, Wednesdays, and Fridays, I cleaned Montrose's studio, changed light bulbs, made his frames, taught him computer tricks, picked up supplies, carried in hamburgers and onion rings or endless cups of coffee. Although he had cut back on sculpture once he began experimenting with computer images, Montrose taught me lost wax casting, how to rubberize molds, how to mix patinas so I could assist with the tiny bronzes he still made. I understood my role immediately: I was his sidekick, his "little assistant," his spy, his conduit to young artists in town, his driver, someone (other than his wife) who could help him answer letters and other difficulties, serve as his witness and advocate, act as the nearest reasonable person who could rephrase or retract his insults. Around him I felt small because he was big in so many ways—the new prints he was making, the huge decision to show again and not as a sculptor, but as a computer artist, the size of his calves, his unending scroll of ideas.

"Montrose's a second class topic," Schuyler said when I first told him that I'd be staying in New Haven. He was merciless. "His art's a time capsule. He can't interest any young artist today." Schuyler had been attacking us both, me—who had deserted him—and my new boss.

Nine months later, he had probably come to the trial to gloat.

"Did Mr. Montrose ever insult you?" Barrow asked Pruhar.

"Yes, he did."

The truth was I loved Pruhar's porcelain and his studio, although I'd never mentioned to Montrose that I'd even visited. In the one finished corner there were glass cases with his pieces laid on red velvet, but the rest of the work space was unfinished; there were grinding machines and mixers and table saws with diamond blades, and on every surface tiny objects were scattered. There were paper lanterns and shells and dominoes and cacti and stained glass and swords and fake flowers. There were throw pillows and agate figurines and scrimshaw and beads. I wanted to touch everything.

"Did there come a time when you stopped being friends?"

"Yes. After the picture appeared in *Vanity Fair*, and the interview, which I should add, I arranged for him."

"The basic issue for the jury is: does this picture or does it not portray Mr. Pruhar," Barrow said. "It seems to me the only way to have the jury make that determination is to show them the plaintiff on the one hand, and permit them to compare him to the computer print published in *Vanity Fair*."

The lawyer took from behind his desk a photographic enlargement—perhaps four feet wide and five feet high—of the *Vanity Fair* picture, and propped it on an easel so that the jury, Pruhar, and the judge could view it; and those of us in the back could see only part of it, sideways.

"Could I ask you, Mr. Pruhar, to describe the picture for us?"

"It's a street scene on a sidewalk at the corner of the building I work in. There is a fountain on the right. There is a traffic sign that seems to have a cherub attached to it on the top, with a cat at its base. The central figure is a partially draped, but otherwise nude young woman, and hiding—I think it's fair to say—behind the corner, and looking in the direction of the young woman with an upraised dagger, is a scowling male figure wearing what almost looks like a sleep mask with eye holes cut in it, and what appears to be a belted overcoat. This figure, as you can see, is me. There is another masked man on the far left who is trying to restrain the knife-bearer."

The "otherwise nude young woman" was Binny, whom I'd called for weeks after the *Vanity Fair* article appeared, trying to apologize. She'd never called me back. I looked across the courtroom to see her reaction to the picture. Rather than looking away, as I guessed she might, her gaze was fixed on it. She did not appear to be embarrassed. She seemed to be measuring Montrose's achievement, trying to decide her value to the work, now visible at a far larger scale than the *Vanity Fair* version. In the courtroom, Binny's beauty was fierce, and the hardness in her eyes made her seem unapproachable. In the picture, the Muse looked wistful, as if misfortune was about to strike.

What Pruhar didn't say was that although Montrose had moved from sculpture to computer, his idiom was the same as the 1970's. His figures had a twisting looseness. Because of this, their faces looked down or turned away from the viewer—particularly the Pruhar figure—concentrating elsewhere. There had never been anything serene about a Montrose piece, and again his artistic vocabulary tended toward sensuous experience, surge and anticipation, the force of the physical world.

Barrow spoke directly to the judge. "This enlargement of the computer image, *The Rape of the Muse* by Harris Montrose, we would like to enter as Exhibit 1. We submit that the figure on the right, despite the fact it has longer hair than Mr. Pruhar has now, is indeed Mr. Pruhar."

42

"Your claim is noted," Judge Miller said.

"Your Honor, if you please, I'd like to submit this item into evidence as Exhibit 2." Barrow handed a large paper bag to Pruhar.

"Now, Mr. Pruhar, I'd like to show you this. Do you recognize this outfit?"

Barrow drew from the bag a blue overcoat.

"Yes, I do."

"Now tell the jury what it is, please?"

"It's one of my favorite coats. I've worn it for about three years."

"Is it your principal winter garment?"

"Yes, it is."

"Do you see anyone wearing that coat in the image of *The Rape of the Muse*?"

"I do."

"Who?"

"It's me."

"The figure holding the knife?"

"Yes."

"Is there anyone else whom you recognize in the picture?"

"Yes. Rand Tabor, Montrose's assistant."

"Would you please—"

"Did I mention that I know the cat?" The crowd giggled.

"Pardon me?"

"I know the cat."

"Would you tell the jury the cat's name?"

"Her name is Scout."

"Who is the owner of the cat you recognize in the picture?"

"Harris Montrose."

Barrow paused again, shuffled his papers. Cynthia, just behind Montrose, stretched, looking concerned.

Everyone without a sense of humor agreed that Montrose was acting out by using Pruhar's likeness in this way. No one quite understood why he turned on his old friend. I had my theories; I wanted to share them with Schuyler now that he'd resurfaced, if we could put our own bad feelings behind us. But why had Pruhar sued? Those who knew him suspected that Pruhar understood the move from sculpture to ceramics was not going to provide the action he needed to feel alive, and the courtroom would.

"Can you tell us what happened the first time you attended an art opening in New York City after the January issue of *Vanity Fair* magazine was published?" Barrow asked.

"It was just after New Year's at the Clementine Stone gallery. There was tremendous commotion when I walked in. I heard scornful laughs as people recognized me. A lot of people had a lot to say to each other and to me about Montrose's picture."

"How long did you remain at that opening?"

"For about an hour."

Having been to a few Boston openings with him, I'd seen Pruhar work an art crowd before. In every encounter, with old acquaintances or strangers, he seemed to offer himself and his services. His great gift was how he played the younger brother role: helpful, unthinkingly selfless. But he was quicker and more intuitive than you'd ever imagine; he was thinking of how the person in front of him might help him someday, what he could ask for in six months. Pruhar was *desperate* to be helpful, make an introduction, make a phone call. The bifocals halfway down his nose helped give him authority. Hanging from a black strap around his neck, they caught themselves when he tossed his hair. While many of his compliments were transparently false, people didn't seem to mind. It was as if strangers expected him in his enthusiastic way to be harmlessly dishonest, an embellisher. He was never penalized for being insincere. Pruhar worked every angle.

"How did you feel when you saw how people were looking at you?"

"Well, I felt humiliated and degraded in front of my colleagues and peers. And it outraged me."

"Did this treatment have any effect on you *after* the opening that night in January?"

"Yes, it did. Every time I thought about it, I got very upset. And my wife was very upset."

"Did you suffer any other ill effects?"

"I lost sleep over it."

"Does this incident at the gallery still trouble you?"

"Yes, it does, and the picture in *Vanity Fair* still troubles me."

"In what respect?"

"Every time I think of it, I'm humiliated again. It constantly runs through my mind, the scorn that Harris Montrose publicly directed at me."

"Have there been other repercussions?"

"Well, I think people have been much more disdainful, and there are some people whom I've heard tell others that they don't want to do business with me because I might be violent."

"Have you ever conducted yourself in a violent manner?"

"No."

"Have you ever attacked anybody?"

"No."

"Have you ever raped anybody?"

"No."

"As an adult, have you had any fistfights?"

"No."

"When was the last time you had any kind of fight?"

"The last one I can remember was when I was eleven, walking home from school. I cracked ice off a bush, and somebody started to pick a fight with me because I was disturbing nature."

Pruhar's gentle voice suggested he'd been a victim here. He seemed a simple man who wanted to make hand-thrown saucers and platters, pitchers and beads. He had asked Montrose for nothing but friendship and he'd been slugged.

❧

I remembered the September morning eight months before the trial when Molly Vidian came to the Abar Lake studio. A month into my job with Montrose, I had been at the studio since seven AM, sweeping and mixing epoxy for the Cengal show only weeks away. Pruhar arrived a half-hour before she did; Pruhar had invited Vidian and he wasn't going to miss her visit, the first magazine interview Montrose had agreed to in twenty-five years.

Montrose usually did not like to have expectant and admiring visitors. Visitors meant effort for him: a tour of the studio while being polite. Still, for some guests he revealed his gentler side. A local art club recently had sent over a group of blue-haired old ladies and Montrose had charmed them with his southern accent. He indulged them, teased them, asked them questions. Montrose had each touch one of his old bronze sculptures. "They don't let you do that in museums," he said cheerfully. For an hour he enjoyed being fawned over and flattered, and he acted shy and modest with them. Near the end, he gave the group an assignment, something to discuss in the van back to the art club. He asked them to name beautiful things, not art items. They left, all smiles, with no idea how challenging Montrose could be.

He always preferred visitors who were willing to quarrel. He liked arguing with feisty classes of students Pruhar brought by. I tried to convince him that his exposure in *Vanity Fair* was a chance to explain his art to a very large class of students: America. He wanted to talk to Vidian about higher things— cultural movements, creativity—but he knew that no reporter from a magazine with a circulation over 100,000 would do that with him; you could lose readers if you got too serious. Pruhar was pushing his comeback, but Montrose wasn't interested in using *Vanity Fair* to talk about himself. Cable and twenty-four-hour news shows had changed things since his success in 1972. Art stars couldn't compete in the media landscape, he believed. When I reminded him that Jackson Pollock had been profiled by *Life* magazine in the 1940's, Montrose said, "He never would have made it on TV."

"Your *Vanity Fair* friend must be peripheral," he called across the room to Pruhar, "writing about art."

"She's not peripheral," Pruhar assured him. "She does profiles of all kinds of celebrities."

"How's my profile?" Montrose asked, turning his head to the side.

I had given Montrose my view that Vidian could have chosen to write on any art subject, painters becoming film directors, the Guggenheim's downtown real estate problem (trustees had been caught using the museum's satellite space to show works they owned as if it were a dealer's back room), or Francis Bacon's long-time gallery defrauding his heirs. But she chose Montrose and I saw this as an exciting augur for his upcoming show.

Ten minutes late, stepping out of a red Citroën convertible, Molly Vidian wore black leggings that emphasized her athletic calves, a yellow blouse with tiny black buttons, and a long black jacket like a Prussian soldier.

Montrose stood when Pruhar went to let her in. When I shook her hand, Molly Vidian smelled like freesia. She had a slender nose and skin that was translucent and slightly downy. The auburn hair piled on top of her head was held in place with long silver needles. She was pretty enough to wake me up a little. I guessed her age to be around forty.

"I wish I knew where the hell all that traffic was going," she said. "Is something big happening around here today?"

"Every day," Montrose joked. "It's a lot like New York here." He shifted back and forth on his feet. His right hand— the hand he might have used to shake hers—was holding the piece of wood he'd been massaging, a sensual habit he used to calm himself.

"You live in a very pretty place," she said.

"Pretty or beautiful?" Montrose asked, starting right in.

She looked over at Pruhar, who had gone to sit on a stool a few feet away, hoping he might interpret this odd question. I wondered for just a moment if she had a sexual relationship with Pruhar, now or sometime in the past.

"And quiet," she said, "once you get off the highway."

"We have a lake," Montrose said, gesturing out the front window with his chin.

"And there's even a television show about your city."

"Have you seen it?" Montrose wanted to know.

"I actually haven't."

"It's nothing much. But my daughter gets a kick out of it."

"You don't watch with her?"

"She lives elsewhere. On a mountaintop. I don't know how she can live at the end of a dirt road. She can't even get through to town in the winter."

"Do you see her often?"

"He's never been to her house," Pruhar said.

"It's very far away," Montrose said. "She was supposed to be here today, but she's not."

"Is she all right?" Pruhar asked. He'd known Lily all her life.

"She's fine. You wouldn't mind if I sat down?" Montrose fell back into his swivel chair. He expected Molly Vidian to take the seat next to the desk, the wax-clotted black canvas chair I usually sat in. He tipped forward and rearranged his tiny piece of wood, ready to drill again. Then he stopped himself, remembering she was here to interview him. "Do you want me to shut the radio off?"

"You should at least turn it down," Pruhar said.

The radio played constantly during my workdays there, and Montrose would shush me from time to time so he could listen. Talk radio, Imus, sports. Talk was the entertainment. "Small time quibbling," he called it.

"Oh now, Cynthia told me not to forget. Can I offer you some coffee, something to drink?"

"Coffee would be wonderful." Her lipstick gave a little pop at the end of her sentences.

"You've already met my little assistant Rand at the door," he said, pointing at me. "He's also excellent at coffee."

"He doesn't look so little to me," she said.

"He knows what I mean," Montrose said.

"I'm going to record, if that's all right?" she said, taking a small black machine from her oversized bag.

"That's all right," Montrose answered.

"Do you mind if I smoke?" she asked.

"God, I'd love to bum a cigarette off of you," he said.

"That's not a problem," she said. I could tell he liked that she smoked. He was jealous.

"You still crave?" Pruhar asked.

"Every minute of every day," Montrose said.

"Don't those Nicorettes help?"

"Are you kidding?" he answered dismissively. Empty cellophane twelve-packs littered his desk.

"How long has it been?" she asked, flicking on her recorder.

"It's been pretty long."

"Have one," she said. "It's really okay to have one."

"Now, you know that's not true. How can you say that to an addict?" He refused her offer.

He seemed in a good mood. I went into the house to get three coffees.

When I returned, I heard Montrose ask Molly Vidian, "What do you got for me?" Now that the radio was quiet and coffee was on the way, he couldn't wait to get going. He wanted to talk art; it was what he lived to talk about.

She curled her back, imitating his posture, flipped open a small red leather-bound notebook and kissed the tip of her pen. He didn't mind that she was flirting with him, trying to charm him. Her presence made me consider how few women visited the studio.

"You live in the city?" he asked aggressively, flirtatiously.

"Yes, I do."

"I was just there."

"Yes. I know. I got a preview of your show."

49

I had also been in New York the week before setting up at the Cengal Gallery. Although I appreciated the city's magnetism, my vision of Manhattan had somehow changed in my month away. The city was all metal and mortar, sharp grit, bite and gears. The back ends of garbage trucks ground and swallowed, a form of violence. Kids clutched schoolbags, women clutched purses, black aides clutched their geriatric employers. The old men at the corners with their greasy hair and fruit juice showed a bright-eyed cruelty toward the pitiable gray birds. In the city, I remembered my first day in New Haven when a blind man in a gray polyester suit crossed the street in front of me just as I turned onto Abar Lake Road. I'd wondered if our contemporaneous arrival had some deeper meaning. He didn't stop at the curb. He just poked forward with his red-tipped stick, walking fast, not caring who was flying toward him. His audacity and fearlessness made me think of him on Fifty-Seventh Street where a cab would have run him down.

"What did you think?" Montrose asked.

"I thought you were worth writing an article about."

"*I* was worth it or the pictures were worth it?"

"I know a lot of people in New York are interested in your return to the scene, and where you've been."

"New York is the center of your ugly art. I don't know if I can participate in that. 'A red square is real, a blue sunset isn't.'"

He was quoting a well-known critic who, he surmised, Molly Vidian might use against him. But she only looked puzzled and amused by his non sequitur.

"I just can't stand that," he said.

"Why not?" She had come suspecting heresy and Montrose would not disappoint her. He presumed that people came to him uneducated, formed only by art world cliché and standard thinking. He assumed art school had taught me nothing; he had a curriculum for me, too. He hadn't finished high school; reading was slow and difficult for him, so he suggested no books: what he needed to teach me was visual. He would start the moment I arrived in the morning. He approved of some of de Kooning, he adored Giacometti; what he didn't like were the thousands of others from Morris Louis on. Pop, Op, Minimalism, neo-Expressionism, Conceptual—the deficient art of the twentieth century. I knew someday he would see and judge my work. If I ever again produced new work.

"There are a lot of people I talk to who believe you can look at a piece of art and take it all in in the blink of an eye. The One Second theory, they call it."

"I've never heard of this. Tell me," she said.

"That's because Harris made it up," Pruhar told her.

"One of the great unforeseen fall-outs of this century," Montrose answered without missing a beat. "Generations of artists who don't look at art."

"Maybe you look for a second if there's only a second's worth of stuff there," Molly Vidian said. "That doesn't sound completely unreasonable."

He actually stopped turning over what he had in his hands and looked up at her. He had a quick take on the shapes of bodies, of hands, of the parts of people. I could tell he thought she was pretty and his southern manners kicked in; this early in the interview he would try not to be overly aggressive. He would try to be instructive.

"Well, then we agree that there should be more than a second's worth in great work."

"But you can get a pretty good idea with just a glance," she suggested.

"What moves people is art that is rich enough, that has enough subtlety and vitality, art that's not used up by a glance."

Interviews are not conversation. The flow of talk is not even. Montrose was impatient with all but a few of her questions, and she was reluctant to let him get off too easily. His views were eccentric, his opinions outrageous. She was probing and nonchalant. He dealt with strangers, even journalists, by trying to shock them. He believed artists should be playful.

"Why don't you show her around?" Pruhar suggested.

Montrose glared at him. "You want me to show you around?"

"Would you?" she asked.

Montrose hauled himself up. Scout had wandered into the studio and leaped onto the pedestal in the corner that held one of the old Biblical sculptures, *The Aftermath*.

"That's a lovely cat," she said.

"He's taken over all the high points in the house," Montrose said. "The pedestals. The mantel over my bed."

"I use a squirt bottle to get my cats out of difficult places," she said, reaching to stroke Scout.

"He just can't learn, poor thing," Montrose said.

"No, really he can. Discipline," she said, hopefully.

"I'm already alienated from him."

He asked who she'd interviewed recently, and she named a famous ballerina, an actor whose career Montrose followed ("I never understood how he made it," Montrose said to me, "his arms are too short."). Montrose asked what kind of art the movie star had in his house and what she thought of him. He liked gossip, he liked to get down and dirty.

I took as a good sign that he kept up a steady patter with Molly Vidian. I thought that Pruhar's recommendation probably protected her.

"Why did you make those Biblical figure groups?" she asked.

"I'm a Southerner. Aren't Southerners known for their love of the Bible?" Montrose teased.

"You're religious?" she asked skeptically.

"He's spiritual," Pruhar said.

"I wanted to do something new," Montrose said.

He had aesthetic reasons for choosing those stories, I knew. He was a reactionary: he wanted to deviate from his 1970's contemporaries' pure interest in form. He wanted to sculpt people. The Bible stories were devices. They allowed for his great spatial breakthrough: he freed figures from the earth. Since the invention of perspective, hundreds of artists had painted *The Descent from the Cross* thousands of times, but no one had sculpted it in the round until Montrose did.

After his 1970's sculpture entered the popular memory, he had seen no reason to repeat himself. It had taken him twenty-five years to come up with something groundbreaking again, and when Nora Cengal called, he was ready to share it. Now how was he going to explain this to Molly Vidian in a way she could use for readers interested in the sex lives of presidential candidates, in the cash of drug cartels, in the slaughter and bones of the latest third world genocide, in mystery and foul play on the Riviera, in Keanu Reeves and Jennifer Lopez?

"How do those Biblical pieces from twenty-five years ago look to you now?" she asked. "They made you famous, after all."

"They look unresolved. Lots of huffing and puffing and not much to show for it. Facility was important to me then. Doing something and making it look easy. But it didn't seem to get easier to make those pieces look more natural. I still wish I had realized them better. I needed someone to say to me, 'Do it right.'"

The best sculptures in the last fifty years and he wanted to realize them better? He was harder on himself than on anyone else. His capacity for work was infinite. That was his lesson; that's what attracted me. I wondered if she would be able to capture it in her article.

"Simon didn't say it?" she asked, pointing her chin at Pruhar.

"Yes. I did," Pruhar said.

"Not often enough," Montrose said. "You know those 100-arm Buddhas they worked on in India for four hundred years and the arms still didn't look right? They couldn't figure out how to do it. They couldn't make the arm insertions correctly. They at least should have come up with something to hide them. Tie a little silk around them."

Molly Vidian laughed a deep, excited, cigarette-loaded sound. I knew her type from parties at Burr's apartment. Well-dressed, aggressively skeptical, but quiet when laying a trap, probably divorced I guessed, with a young daughter who was given exorbitant birthday parties in Central Park, twenty-five six-year-old kids invited for pony rides and lunch at Tavern on the Green and a four hundred dollar cake to make up for mommy's long working hours and the Barbadian nanny.

"When I did my Biblical figures, people said, 'They look too much like art.' What they meant was: these are figures we recognize so they can't be original. And everyone agrees that in the twentieth century originality is the measure. But art should set out to be beautiful, not necessarily original. If you're only into original, what you get is Jeff Koons. Basketballs half-floating. They mean nothing to me. Stainless steel soldiers. Less than nothing. Fifty years from now, museum space will get to be at a premium and they'll stop putting that shit up."

"So what's beautiful now?" she asked.

"I don't know," Montrose replied. If you didn't know him, you might think he was being coy, that he was being falsely modest, that he couldn't say simply, 'My work and no other is beautiful'; you might think that's what he wanted to say. I wasn't surprised that he had no easy answer for Ms. Vidian.

At that moment I thought of Binny, who was also a journalist. I thought of her delicate happy face and long teeth with which she bit up the universe. I wondered how she worked during her interviews. I could imagine Binny Sanford taking on one of the slick young music industry point men she'd told me about. After one conversation I knew how she felt about the industry; she saw it as something separate from the young naïve bands she covered. In the six weeks since we'd met, she'd sent me an article she'd done on one of the industry scouts whose job was to write the first deal memos that locked a new band into legal hell. The scouts used meaningless jargon to make young guitarists think they were simpatico. There was a line of Binny's I remembered clearly. "Every time they used a word like 'punchy' or 'warm' or 'groove' or 'vibe,' I wanted to throttle somebody."

"Let's talk about the arc of your career," Molly Vidian said, getting no traction on the beauty question.

"You shouldn't want to talk about that," Montrose said.

"Why not?"

"There isn't much arc. We should talk about what's happening now."

"People will want to know where you've been," she said, referring to her notes.

"I've been working."

"But not at your career. That's what's so unusual here." Montrose had no fear of obsolescence. He felt he had done all he could do in three dimensions. He moved to the computer so that he did not have to repeat what he'd done before.

I remembered Pruhar telling me he hadn't been overly concerned when Montrose moved into computers, although he was worried that critics wouldn't believe computers had anything to say about art, then or in the future.

"Let me tell you a story about someone I know," Montrose said. "I think it's a fairly typical story and has a lesson in it. When this guy first went to New York he was pushing himself to be an important sculptor. That didn't work, and he came here. He worked a little, but mostly he tried to keep his connections in New York alive. He developed a situation based on reciprocals; you help me, I'll help you. He taught art. His students were the children of famous people, politicians, rock stars. He was able to leverage situations through his teaching job. It took a certain talent. He didn't have much going, but his reciprocals gave him a little bit of a scene. Every few years he had a show in New York with a little review in the back of *ARTnews* and magazines like that. Back of the magazine snippets. It was all insider stuff, you know, like 'couldn't put up an ugly painting if he tried.'"

"So he worked on his career," she said.

On his stool, Pruhar grew unsettled. He started pulling at his ear as if he weren't hearing right. Then I understood that

Montrose was talking about *him*. I wondered if Molly Vidian knew. The details thus far had been vague; the unnamed guy could have been one of any number of artists. Pruhar said nothing. He didn't want to give himself away.

"The gaps remained enormous," Montrose said.

"The gaps?"

"Between who was hot and who wasn't. All of his work on his career was just diversionary. It didn't grow to anything. And if he had stopped pushing for one hour, it would have all imploded."

"Did he know that?" she asked.

"He knew."

"But he tried anyway."

"It's what he had," Montrose said, disparagingly. "And sometimes it seemed to work out. Last year, he was supposed to have some things in a Cleveland art museum show. But then that didn't work out."

"Why not?"

"He says it was because the curator was fired."

"And that was the end of his show?"

"Things are very flimsy in this world." Montrose sounded disappointed. I didn't understand why he was going after Pruhar. The attack was cruel; Montrose's mean streak was wide. What had Pruhar done?

"You look down on what he was doing, trying to keep himself present in New York, don't you?" She looked up to speak, pausing in her note-taking.

"Yes, I do."

"Why?"

"He should have been working."

"It sounds, from what you've told me, as if he was productive, a show every few years," Molly Vidian offered.

"His networking took five hours a day."

"Was that a problem?"

Montrose's face twisted in irritation.

56

"It's about where your head is. Even when he was sculpting, he was plotting. In a way, his sculptures were like plots. They were systems."

"What did you want from him?" I cut in. All of a sudden, Montrose's standards seemed too high to me. The hopes for my career were under attack too.

"I wanted him to stop carrying himself as if his lesser work was significant. That's all."

Montrose continued. "Then, through his college teaching, he met the son of a famous entrepreneur. One of those men who build a fortune selling dinnerware and flatware and glassware, things that you wear. The man branches off into accessories, home furnishings and decor. Through the son, who happens to be a student in one of his classes, this artist gets to the man and convinces him to go into ceramics, there's money in ceramics if it's done right, done artistically.

"I actually believe that this artist is one of those people who's blown his gifts."

Pruhar still didn't give himself away. By her lack of response, Molly Vidian obviously didn't know that Pruhar made ceramics.

There was a long, awkward silence. Then the conversation bounced to other subjects—the red Citroën in the driveway, *Vanity Fair*'s advertising base, whether she was a Knicks fan— and finally back to art with Montrose spouting, "Impressionism is like color photography, no cultural barriers. It's easy to love. But it's soft love.

"I just heard that the Japanese fellow who paid $82 million for a Van Gogh died and had the painting buried with him. You should write about him. Now that's an art story!"

"There's a man who loved art," Molly Vidian agreed.

"He did it so his heir wouldn't have to pay inheritance tax," Montrose reported.

"Sounds like something you'd do," Pruhar said. I wondered whether he was retaliating for the story Montrose had just told on him.

"We haven't talked yet about your early years," she said. His inheritance remark must have reminded Vidian of her research about his father's money and the fight over it. I knew from Pruhar that Montrose hadn't spoken to his brother in years. "Your mother? What did she do?"

"She cut roses in our garden. She wore long white gloves and carried a basket over her arm."

"She wasn't an artist?"

"She knew artists."

"And your father was a businessman." Pruhar had warned Montrose that Molly Vidian dug deep on her subjects, interviewed childhood friends, called around, found the full biography.

"My father eventually crushed the businesses of people who didn't take him seriously."

"He was vengeful."

"He didn't suffer disappointments."

Montrose never spoke of his father, although Pruhar did. Pruhar had met Julius Montrose once in New Orleans in the 1970's, and described him as a volatile man in a seersucker suit. He'd been impressed by the senior Montrose's manicured fingernails, his energy and suspiciousness. Harris had been cocky in the old days, Pruhar liked to tell me; Julius Montrose took great pleasure in putting his son in his place.

"He was very successful though, wasn't he?" Molly Vidian continued.

"He had his fun," Montrose answered. "He was a dealmaker with high blood pressure. The rest you should look up. Tell me what you find."

Although he wouldn't speak more of his father's businesses, he wanted to talk about wealth. He wanted Molly Vidian to explain the Internet to him. He didn't really understand what it was, how to get there, what he might find.

"Maybe America doesn't need art now that we have the Internet," Montrose announced.

At the end of the morning, I was certain she didn't *get* Montrose. Who could understand a man who dismissed abstract art, demanded beauty, and didn't care who liked his work today as long as people liked it 100 years from today? Who could make sense of a man who had no favorite restaurants, who belonged to no clubs or organizations, who never traveled, and wasn't sure he would make the opening of his first New York show in thirty years. Still, I guessed her article would be flattering; it was her job to make him fascinating.

❧

"Mr. Pruhar, have you in any of your work as a painter or sculptor used allegories, for instance, painted in the form of allegory?" Pontes began the cross-examination.

"Well, do you mean by that a mythic subject?" Pruhar was sitting up straighter now.

"Have you ever utilized allegory as a vehicle for presenting some of your work?"

Barrow rose, bearlike. "I object to the form of that question, your Honor."

"Well, if the artist does not understand it, he should tell us," Judge Miller said.

"I don't understand it," Pruhar said.

"Okay. Do you know what an allegory is?" Pontes asked.

"I'll tell you the truth. I always mistake it for a metaphor, so I'm not exactly clear," Pruhar answered weakly, embarrassed.

"Okay. Let me ask you to presume for the purpose of the examination for the next few moments that an allegory is an expression, by means of symbolic fictional figures and actions, of truths or generalizations about human existence. Now, did you ever paint or sculpt, given that definition, an allegorical form?"

"I would say, given that definition of representational art, there *is* no other form." His eyes were like two solitary sparks overshadowed by black eyebrows. In those eyes were concentrated all Pruhar's intelligence and deep cunning.

"Does Mr. Montrose make images in allegorical form?"

"Yes. Everybody . . . You can't . . . by that definition, every imagined work is an allegory."

"Do many of Mr. Montrose's images use symbols in them?"

"Yes." His head bobbed slowly.

"Have you ever adopted symbols in any of your work to represent ideas that you were trying to convey?"

"Yes."

"Did you ever discuss the use of symbols in art with Mr. Montrose as a means of conveying an artist's expression?"

"I'm sure I did at some point."

"Were these heated discussions?"

Pruhar's mouth tightened. "I don't recall."

"Okay. What position in those discussions did you take concerning the use of symbols in paintings?"

Barrow stood. "Objection, your Honor. This is irrelevant. Mr. Pruhar can't be expected to remember conversations on a subject he's had to have defined for him."

"This is cross-examination and counsel may proceed on the general subject of symbols and allegorical references," Judge Miller said. "Restate your question."

"What was your position in discussions with Mr. Montrose regarding the use of symbols in paintings?" Pontes asked.

"I can't recall exactly."

"Mr. Pruhar, what is a muse?"

"One of the daughters of Zeus, who was created to protect the arts."

"All right. Are most artists familiar with the use of the symbol of the muse?"

"Some would be, and some wouldn't be, I suppose."

"Did you ever do any work in which you depicted a muse?"

"I can't think of any of my own."

"But many artists are familiar with the use of the symbol of the muse, as far as you know?"

"Yes."

"And when the *Vanity Fair* picture appeared it had a title did it not? Typed right across the picture: *The Rape of the Muse?*"

"Yes."

"Are you familiar with many of Mr. Montrose's works?"

"Yes, I am."

"Am I correct in saying that he used allegories in some of his famous Biblical pieces?"

"You are correct."

"No further questions, your Honor."

I looked over at Montrose. His face registered no elation. His jowls slumped; his eyes were funereal. We all stood when the judge left the room. Montrose stood, then fell back into his chair with an exhausted old-guy sigh. He was overtired, impatient to get home, back to his cats and the quiet of his studio.

I looked across the room for Schuyler. I wanted to catch up, if only to report to Melanie that he was okay. But he was gone.

CHAPTER 4

The work Molly Vidian had seen before her visit to New Haven was a preview of the "Wrestling" show at the Cengal Gallery on Fifty-Seventh Street. I had finished arranging Montrose's work on the walls there (his entrusting me with this job made me feel modest) just in time to make it back for the interview at Abar Lake.

My return to the city that week had made me madly excited. Just setting foot in New York brought good luck it seemed. Soho was riding on the back of Wall Street, a runaway colt. The stock market had been hot for a decade bubbling up IPOs, and New Yorkers were constantly thirsty for quick profits and cool microbrew beer, drinking open-mouthed wherever you turned. The Dow was at 10,000, and Nasdaq was breaking records daily. I'd missed the city's decadence which to me had always been a matter of opposites: the acres of glass inviting stares during the day and the rolled down armor covering them at night, the silence of limos and the blasting taxi horns of rush hour, the cool air in hotel lobbies and the baking sidewalks, the blond boys in blazers waiting with their nannies at the Met when I arrived for work in the morning, and the Hispanic kids outside my old apartment shirtless at the refreshing stream of the fire plug in the evening.

In this final season of the millennium, New York was filled with installations, panty-strewn chandeliers, and artists who caged themselves as rabid dogs. There were feminist landscapes,

xeroxed found items, videos of wallpaper, the novelty of minia-
tures, blow-ups of architectural drawings, psyschosexual dramas,
photographic parodies of the dominatrix. There was messianic
art and a few Monochromes and modern Chinese painting still
unsure about using Western perspective. Conceptual Art was
over, said the critics, but it was everywhere in the Village.

Once I'd met Nora Cengal, I understood she did nothing
without a sense that she might succeed. She was tiny, with
profuse dark hair and pale green eyes, a severe South American beauty, strong-boned and dark-skinned. Having worked
in her space for two days, I'd come to see that she did most of
her business on the phone, walking from corner to corner of
the gallery. A headset framed her Velasquez face as she spoke
into her chiclet-sized mouthpiece in Spanish to Bogota and
Lima, Buenos Aires and Madrid. Although I knew no Spanish,
I could tell Nora Cengal was impatient, flattering, difficult to
refuse. On the verge of a deal, she would disappear behind the
door to her office. If a sale fell through she would come out
and walk over to the window, silently looking down six floors
to the street, watching the unruly life crisscrossing below as if
she were thinking of jumping. Then the curses would start to
fly. "Puta, pendejo, idiotas."

She treated her clients as innocents, the ones who actually
came to look at what they were buying. Sitting them on the
white sofas in the middle of the gallery, she would lightly touch
their wrists if they were men, their knees if they were women.
Nora would pretend to brush lint from her skirt. She would
offer seltzer in blue bottles and propose a toast, "To Beauty." I
wanted her to represent my work to the world.

She dressed in expensive suits to which she pinned jewels,
but she wore no rings. I wondered if she kept a man at home
who threw on a condom when she privately felt at a loss, who
fed her snacks (she never ate in the days I was there), who
handed her the headset when inspiration struck. The Cengal
business was booming.

"I believe that Beauty is making a comeback in New York," she'd said to Montrose during their first phone call. Although he had never heard of Nora or her gallery, he said he had nothing to worry about from a woman who could say something like that out loud. It was a line he had repeated to me for weeks, shaking his head. Montrose believed in Beauty too. He believed that it was a vehicle for Big Ideas, and all great artists had Big Ideas. Rubens: The world is awash in natural forms. Rodin: The human nude is the temple of the sensual world. Giacometti: man's isolation can be seen through Scale. Montrose believed art had to take up Big Ideas that dealt with formal questions, questions that other arts, such as writing, couldn't take up. Like perspective. "You could try, but you could never really *describe* perspective," Montrose used to say. "That's what makes it *our* work. Everyone says Rothko took up ecstasy and despair, but those never seemed like particularly visual themes to me."

Of course, Nora didn't know the day Montrose called back to accept her offer that he might not show up for his own opening. He hadn't shown up in 1972, and he'd been ambivalent about coming to the city even before Vidian's visit. When I called him in New Haven to describe the gallery—the two large rooms with wide plank floors, the sunlight of Fifty-Seventh Street—he said, "They'll want me to chat. I really don't chat well." If he'd told Nora during his acceptance call that he wouldn't attend the opening, she wouldn't have believed him. I wouldn't have either.

She had asked him for six PM on the night of the opening, but he hadn't arrived by the time the handsome, kissing gallery crowd in New York began to arrive at Cengal just after seven. I recognized many of them from my former life. I put them into categories: people in a hurry, people who laughed too loud, those who prowled and coveted ties, shoes, glasses, hairstyles, fabulous legs. To get here they had already fought through a migraine, a traffic jam, two changes of clothes, and last-minute doubt.

Every artist under thirty had been promoted and used and excluded and undone by someone in the room, and each approached these Friday events with glossy fear. Every artist over forty had been reviewed and photographed, and later thought irrelevant. But they came out to be discovered again. Some held back just as they came in, ready for defeat. They all knew they looked good. Thin belts over flat bellies. Narrow ties beside thin lapels. They were ecstatic seeing each other—kissing again and again. A few kissed me, said they hadn't seen me around much; they tried to talk to me but I didn't feel like talking, I was too nervous.

Those who stopped to look around at the work in the first room took deep breaths. Somehow, Montrose had managed to make his vines and trees, posed like humans, sexier than nudes. Kudzu had been transformed into wrestlers, the flexed backs of men. Viewers felt the shaky pleasure of seduction. The jet-ink prints caught surface texture so that bark revealed secret human places and hidden lines. Wind tugged at Montrose's emotional figures, limbs arced against gray skies. His combative vine-women were awkward, off-balance, the tree-men heroic. In these compositions Montrose laid claim to the history of Western art.

It was warm for the first weekend in October, and the front door to the gallery was open. A small bar stood in the corner attended by a sleek hovering man in a vivid black and white checked shirt. He had lined up glasses of white and red wine across the surface. I took a Chardonnay and asked the bartender to top me off.

Only over-enthusiasm offered a chance of survival in New York City; those with the slightest hint of self-surrender were peremptorily extinguished. Back in the city, I heard my old abrasive, goading voice in the people around me; I saw them checking their outfits in the reflecting windows of this heaven and hell of elegance. The gallery light glittered. A few burned with triumph, found their positions quickly, and held forth, well-informed and cagey. One told another about the Francis

Bacon show up the street, the paintings framed in gold leaf at $5,000 per. A soft-looking man with old eyes, a little drunk already, admitted, "I can't have a career." When I was picked by the *New York Times* in their annual celebration of new artists "to watch," I had learned to smile at everyone and everything, to be non-controversial; I was amazed to discover that I no longer had a feeling of kinship for my fellow painters and sculptors. A season away had refreshed and sharpened my vision.

Watching the crowd filing into the Cengal Gallery, I realized that even for those who had never heard of him before the show, the story of Montrose's withdrawal and reemergence made this event irresistible. Perhaps I had underestimated the scope of his legend. Hidden in Connecticut, Montrose's distance gave him an unassailability, burnished his image. He refused to cultivate art columnists, but his myth was intact among those interested in representing the human body.

The day of the opening, inquiring calls to the gallery tripled. Little do they know how beautiful his new pictures are I thought as the phone rang again and again. The computer prints stiffened the hairs on the back of my neck. Don't settle for too little, his pictures said. Modern art had lost all interest in Beauty, and would soon be reassigned to second-rate status where it belonged, Montrose believed. He had been drilling this line into me. The bloodless veneration of ugly modern art only made him surer of himself.

The show attracted some odd audiences. Nora Cengal had advertised in *Computerworld*, and besides the art crowd there were the computer geeks who must have seen in Montrose's prints an expression of their own secretive, imprisoned hallucinatory souls. Adobe Photoshop was kindergarten to them, but they sensed that Montrose—whom they had never met, never heard of—had turned to their technology to make his new mark. Unlike artists, computer folks had a feel for myth. The advertising types had come out too, learning of the show through their Information Services staff, the guys who kept the operating systems running on Madison Avenue. Wearing black, the admen were fixated on finding images of Montrose's they could use to sell product in the next campaign. And the admen told their girlfriends and their clients, and their girlfriends told *their* girlfriends, and the idea of a cyber art show seemed brilliant, sensationally inventive on an October night.

Did I imagine Binny would actually show up? How would I account for it if she did? I knew almost nothing about her; she knew almost nothing about me. It was difficult to believe that I had come to New York as an insider at the most interesting show of the decade, and yet was hopelessly distracted by a woman I'd met once and hadn't seen in over a month.

Pruhar, wearing a large bracelet of burnished silver—his own design—arrived alone, entering the gallery slowly, cautiously, as if he were a foreigner who didn't know the customs. I watched him anonymously circle the brightly lit rooms, studying Montrose's pieces, which he had seen a hundred times, but also studying who was in the gallery, mapping the vortex of the party. He wore a loose black silk jacket over a T-shirt and white cotton pants, clothes that were modest and creased. He was pleased to be thin; he was a boy who happened to have gray hair. At the age of forty-nine Pruhar was not light on his feet, which had calcium spurs that caused him to grimace. If I didn't know better, I would have taken him for a lady's man, a gallery visitor who was on the lookout for any beautiful woman who seemed half-willing to listen to his undeniably smooth voice and to look into his dark eyes. Pruhar was alluring; Montrose swore his friend had never cheated on his wife of almost thirty years, his high school girlfriend who didn't attend art events.

When Pruhar found me, he poured it on. "The pieces look great. You did this just right, and I bet Nora didn't even notice. It takes an artist to appreciate how you've hung this." He put his glasses on and took them off again. "How's it been here, back in your old city?"

In the days following Montrose's anonymous attack on Pruhar in front of Molly Vidian, I wondered how they got along at all. Their lives had been parallel, although Pruhar's needs were more extreme. He reveled in attention. Vain, he suffered the cycles that Montrose avoided—pursuit of fame, modest success, sudden and unexpected neglect, and pursuit again. Even in the months I'd known him, his moods swung wildly. A new fascination with glass and its possibilities as a material turned into irrational despair over not being asked to judge a local glassworks competition. He was always suffering some insult which perhaps explained how he recovered so easily from Montrose's barbs and remained a good friend.

"Where's Harris?"

"Not here yet," I reported.

"When did you last hear from him?"

"He called from New Haven this morning."

"And . . ."

"I'm not sure he's coming at all."

"He'll be here. He's just trying to be dramatic." He paused. "On the other hand, I know Cynthia had to go away suddenly. Her mother went into the hospital. Without Cynthia's help he might not be able to get himself out of the house. I offered to drive him but he refused."

He touched the bridge of his glasses. "How's the shop she runs here, Nora?"

He spoke in low tones, in confidence. He was always willing to consider jumping galleries if the right offer came along, if he could make the right deal happen. Montrose would either come to the opening or he wouldn't; Pruhar had his own business to attend to.

"She likes to sell."

"Montrose thinks she's interested in aesthetics, you know. But if you look at her, you know she really appreciates a good bid."

"He thinks everyone is interested in aesthetics."

Pruhar was susceptible to money, although fame was what he schemed for. He courted critics. Here on Fifty-Seventh Street with the air smelling of lipstick and the sweetness of gay men's cologne, with Manhattan turning dark and throaty just outside the door, he felt close to celebrity and to big spenders. He was a capitalist who just happened to be an artist. He'd set himself a challenge for the evening: figure out the Cengal Gallery, figure where it fit in the constellation of prosperous galleries. He wasn't here to meet artists, or to talk to old friends like Burr, whom he only saw a few times a year; he was scouting. Pruhar wanted to be able to report to Montrose where he, Montrose, had landed, whether this Nora Cengal had long-term prospects in the business.

Pruhar left me to make another circuit of the gallery. He was calculating the best way to approach Nora Cengal and get the inside dope. His game was far more subtle than simple support of Montrose. He wanted to help Montrose to make progress, and along the way help himself.

The two women painters from last month's lecture came in. The older, taller one led the younger who, with jowls and a white-fringed helmet haircut, looked ruthless and bitter. Just behind them, Burr entered the gallery, picked off a glass of red wine, and spotted me. He wore brown corduroy pants and a tweed jacket. His eyes were streaked like old yellow marbles.

Close up, Burr smelled like chocolate cake. "Last night, I dreamed I was in the Olympics, some running event, and I came in third. What does that say about my ambition?"

"That you're ready to train four more years," I teased.

"How are you adjusting to New Haven anyway?" he asked. But before I had a chance to answer he said, "That place is a graveyard with lights. Nobody who lives there has ever been downtown. And they're proud of that. You can't live in such a place. How can you live in a city with a center that consists of a bus depot? It's sad enough that Montrose is there."

Unlike Montrose who loved many things—the New England Patriots, jelly donuts, the feel of mink—Burr was essentially negative, sardonic, an enthusiast of blame.

Burr put one of his famous albino hands (they lacked pigment nearly to the wrist) around my shoulder. "Did you invite the spice rack?"

"I did, but it doesn't mean she's coming."

I'd read the few articles she'd sent, we'd spoken a few times, she'd become an insidious part of my daydreams, but I didn't know what Binny's apartment was like, what neighborhoods she prowled, what television shows she liked, whether she used two pillows or one, whether she slept late or woke up early. Would I have been so interested in her if she hadn't been beautiful, if I hadn't seen her Achilles tendon? I thought of flirting with her at the lecture; I'd always loved to flirt. I loved its uncertainty, its deferrals and light touch of cruelty, the way you could use it to play for time while trying to figure out your intent and opportunities. The way Binny flirted back was a sign she desired a certain kind of torture. But if she didn't accept my invitation to the opening, I didn't expect to see her again.

"Where's our hero?" Burr asked. He was sentimental in the New York way, with its culture of bums, legends, and fallen idols.

"No one knows if he's coming," I said.

"He's an asshole if he doesn't. Every twenty-five years he can make the effort."

Burr saw some of his students, and when he wandered off I forced myself to mingle. I moved to congratulate Nora Cengal. But as I approached, one of her staff whispered to her and she hurried off in the other direction. A moment later she came out of her office walking toward me with a phone in her hand.

"It is your boss," she said, handing me the receiver. It was nearly eight o'clock and Montrose was in the Tuscany Hotel two blocks away. He needed me to come over.

When he let me into Room 434, Montrose was wearing an undershirt and gray slacks. He seemed agitated, his reading glasses dangling from his neck. "I don't understand what Cynthia packed for me," he said. Then he handed me the Weekend

Arts section of the *New York Times*. "It's easier for me if you read," he said. He threw himself onto the bed, stretching out. The television was on, CNN's nightly business report. Montrose picked wax from his ear with a match.

In the article Montrose had chosen, the art critic offered an overview of six downtown shows under the heading, "New Styles of the Season." Montrose's opening was not listed. After I read two sentences, Montrose announced he was against Style. "A discussion of differences," he called it contemptuously. "Style is about process—how we got to this or that point—it's conceptual. It's the product of art historians and their ordering of differences. The only interesting discussion of art is why a piece works or doesn't work.

"If the impetus for your art is to make a new style, imagination suffers," Montrose said. "You don't throw out the old just to service the new. It's wasteful. Yet it's what we've done continuously for the last fifty years. Throw it out just because we're supposed to? So we can have something new?"

He drank from a can of classic Coke that he held against his cheek between sips. His chest was pale, a few gray hairs poking out of his V-neck. He had deep lines from the corners of his mouth curving toward his chin that gave him a sadness his upturned lips couldn't make up for. The suitcase Cynthia had packed was unopened on the chair across the room.

"The gallery is crowded," I told him. "Why don't you go over?"

"They've got my pictures, they don't need me," he said. "What's in it for me over there?"

What a time for him to go invisible! How could he? Was he being dramatic, or was he intimidated by all the attention? Although he seemed fearless in his studio—expressing his views wildly, guided by instinct—lying on his bed here he seemed unsure. He looked like he was suffering.

I couldn't hold back my impatience. "How about meeting your dealer? How about meeting your fans? How about seeing Pruhar and Burr?"

Montrose ignored my suggestions. He drove the match deep into his ear and slowly twisted it, talking on about the review I'd just read to him. I knew all this art talk was a way of distracting himself, of avoiding more immediate demands.

"I think you should go to the opening now," I said.

"What about your friend Schuyler, did he come?" Montrose asked. He often wanted to discuss my friends and Schuyler in particular. He'd predicted that Schuyler wouldn't come to the opening. Montrose enjoyed reviewing people's base instincts and self-interest. He was on the lookout for hypocrites, and he thought he'd found one in Schuyler. But at this moment his interest was merely a stalling tactic.

"No."

"Of course he didn't."

"Pruhar said you'd hesitate, that you'd hide in New Haven or your hotel, that you'd be afraid of coming," I threw back at him.

Montrose put the Coke down on the bedside table. "He won't mind a few minutes alone with Nora Cengal. He'll find her and try to convince her to have a ceramics show, and then we'll have to hear how close-minded she is when she refuses. Simon works all the angles and doesn't even know he's doing it."

"You're no good at the angles?" I asked. Working at his career meant asking for favors, which Montrose wouldn't do. Maybe this show felt like he was asking a favor.

I opened his suitcase and withdrew a black silk shirt. When he stood I helped him button it, and then he sat on the bed and put on his white sneakers. I handed him his belt and jacket.

On the way over, Montrose noticed the second story gyms on Madison where women in black spandex stared down at us from their treadmills. He commented on the number of police patrolling the street. He told me that despite the notorious sexual assault against an immigrant by cops in a station house in Brooklyn, racism in New York was nothing compared to New Orleans. Then he went back to art. He talked about Jasper Johns' *White Flag* ("Aren't you for nationalism?"

he teased. "But then again, what's a flag without its colors?"), and about his favorite sculptor as a youth, Marino Marini, who made muscular horses and riders. His curriculum for me in New Haven was not contemporary—Rubens, Michelangelo, Giacometti, the *Venus of Dusseldorf*. He had urged me to check out Géricault; he had a taste for the early storm scenes of Turner. He liked things in motion: clouds, animals, vines, wrestlers. When I looked at his pictures side-by-side in the gallery, I'd seen hints of all his favorites. Montrose, without a GED, knew art like a second language.

When she saw us, Nora hurried to open the door for Montrose. They had never met. Montrose had brought his red can of Coke which he held with two fingers. The Coke meant he was still a little dry-mouthed, but now his wet lips were humorous; he wasn't interested in dignity. He gave her a weak smile.

Nora was delighted. "Many people have expressed great interest in your work already," I heard her say.

"Tell me what you mean by that, and remember I'm slow," he said charmingly. She told him two newspaper critics had been by, and a collector from Toronto.

Behind Montrose, a group of men wearing alligator boots and llama coats appeared at the door, one young handsome man accompanied by larger young men, his bodyguards. One of them had a German shepherd. I figured them for a private security force. I watched Nora pass Montrose into the crowd, then she opened the door again and kissed the cheeks of the handsome figure at the center of the llama coats. Nora Cengal led her important guest (more important obviously than Montrose, who just supplied the product) inside and around the circumference of the room holding onto his arm. He was a wide-shouldered and bullish man with an arrogant forehead and leather pants. They were a handsome couple, exotic. His hair glistened and was as dark as his eyes. Nora's accented banter was easy and confident and a little childish in the midst of the show's excitement. She gave the impression that she was only making suggestions to her friend, but I could tell she was trying to lead him to higher things. By breeding and temperament Nora Cengal was bound to the finer world, leatherpants knew. I wondered where she came from, what wealth started her off. When he stopped to study a picture, she did as well. Nora had to pretend to be obedient to her powerful collector who, I figured, was as likely to be murdered over cocaine distribution routes in the next month as to arrange for his living room to be redone.

"The pieces look good," Montrose said to me. "Too bad there are all these people in the way."

"You should be happy they came," Nora said catching up to us, mid-tour. "A tribute to your Beauty."

Burr came over to join our little circle.

"Did you get my happy birthday song on your answering machine last week?" Montrose asked him. He started to sing again, "Happy birthday to you, Happy birthday to you, Happy birthday dear . . ."

"Yes, I did."

"I thought of it myself."

"How was your drive?" Burr asked. I'd once heard Montrose say that the only reason to drive in New York was to cut off a few cabs.

Montrose ignored the question. "I have a read on those thirty-nine people who did that mass suicide in California," he began. Cult members had recently poisoned themselves and were found on the floor of their compound in Pomona—it was all over the news.

I knew he would prefer to talk about anything other than his pieces, and his show.

"If you study modern art you could have predicted it," Montrose continued.

"Really," Burr said skeptically.

"Modern art advocated it in a way. After all, modern art, if it stands for anything, stands for the need for a non-material world. Abstract art is a denial of the palpable world. So of course there are these people who leave their bones behind. Who needs bodies?"

"That's it?" Burr asked. "That's your whole theory?"

"I see everything through a filter, don't I?" Montrose said. He spoke like a crazy tyrant and he didn't care what people thought. He sipped his Coke and ran his hand through his thick graying hair.

When Nora circled back, she pulled her collector into our circle. "This is Alex Samon. Alex has a private museum in Lima." He gave Montrose a bear hug, and Montrose, one hand caught over the young man's shoulder, squeezed his can, denting it. Close up, I saw that Samon had a look that said he could be your master if he so desired, but he would do anything for Nora.

"You are working very hard," Samon said to Montrose, thickly rolling his r's.

"You are too," Montrose answered. "I like your shoes."

Samon looked down at his boots, then up, modestly.

"I will send you a pair from Barcelona."

"You really should," Montrose replied. I'd never seen Montrose in anything but sneakers.

"Alex believes that your work has a South American element," Nora said.

"Tell him he's correct," Montrose said. He had to be joking. Samon looked pleased by the compliment.

"You know, I used to try to figure out how this art market works—who buys what and how they decide it's worth the risk—but I gave up. You can't get a straight story from anyone," Montrose said to Burr over his shoulder.

When Samon excused himself to take a phone call, Pruhar approached looking very serious. "So you made it."

Montrose grunted.

Pruhar took Montrose's elbow and guided him to one of the newer pieces, one he'd never seen before. I followed. There seemed to be no hard feelings between them after the Vidian visit.

"I like where this one's going," Pruhar said, pointing. They were the same age, he and Montrose, although not in the same physical condition. Montrose never exercised and Pruhar owned a treadmill. He had a healthy rosy color to him. Montrose's eyes were puffy, the pouches heavy.

"Where's it going?"

"A new direction."

"I'm not so sure."

When Montrose slipped away from Pruhar I followed, dodging the currents of cologne, the smell of white cheese on toothpicks, hoping to pick up the sweet scent of ginger, of Binny.

"Why didn't you ever live in New York?" I asked him.

"Oh my God, that's a question. That's the hardest question you've ever asked me. It's not even like I almost did. I didn't. If you move to New York, you're 100 percent career, and I think I knew even early on how abrasive that psychology would be. I think early on I knew better."

"Plenty of people manage to make good art in this city," I said defensively. I knew I'd move back sooner or later.

"There's no high road here. There's no pretending you're not here purely for your career. One hundred percent career or you develop a rash."

A small tanned man wearing purple shorts, with muscular hairless calves, came up beside Montrose. He was drinking red wine. "I have one drink and it goes to my head," he said. He wore a white, collarless linen shirt. "How about you, do you drink?"

"Coke," Montrose told him, lifting the can.

"I'm sorry I don't have any to offer you."

Montrose was silent.

"You're the artist, aren't you?"

"For tonight."

"I'm very fond of your work. New York is filled with amateurs."

76

"Those aren't amateurs, they're failed artists," Montrose said, inching away.

"You haven't sold many tonight, have you?"

"No. But I didn't expect to." I could see Montrose wanted to shut him off, but couldn't.

"Yes, you did," the man said, aggressively, his hands on his hips. "You're kidding, aren't you? You should have sold them all," he said, and ran his fingers across his buzzed-down hair. The man bumped shoulders flirtatiously with Montrose and began laughing, clearly a little drunk.

"Would you like to get out of here with me?" the man asked.

"Why would I?" Montrose said angrily.

"You seem the type who deserves to be treated well. You might like it if you tried."

He put his arm around Montrose's shoulder. He went on tiptoe, leaned his head toward Montrose and kissed him on the cheek.

Montrose wheeled and grabbed the man's shirt and shoved him hard. The man's head snapped back and his muscular legs worked hard to catch his body, but he staggered back toward a patch of white wall and hit it hard, just between two large frames.

Montrose looked over to me as his witness. His eyes were dark, dilated with excitement. His face was red. Behind me, it was suddenly silent. Everyone was watching.

It seemed only fitting that this show "Wrestlers" included its own wrestling match. That Montrose had handled another man roughly would have surprised no one who knew his many visceral reactions—his fury with other drivers, his hatred of the Patriots' coach who punted on fourth-and-one rather than go for the first down. Montrose was a man of deep feelings and impulse, and he was not above savagery.

The man brushed his shirt off, started to walk toward the exit. Samon and his gangsters regarded Montrose with a certain amused admiration. The fight—or shove—only contributed to Montrose's mystique as far as they were concerned.

They would have preferred an all-out riot with baseball bats I guessed. But I knew that now there would be some sales.

As the crowd began to settle back, Montrose announced to everyone, to no one in particular, "It's a mistake to look to artists for lifestyle guidance." He smiled. I remembered how he chest-bumped me in the atrium to his studio during my first visit.

Nora Cengal rushed over to apologize.

"When he tried to kiss me, I should have bitten into his cheek and held on and shook my head back and forth until he screamed," Montrose told her. He was perspiring like an offensive guard just out of the game.

"This is not good for your show," Nora said.

"It's not so bad," Montrose said. "Rand is always telling me that the art world in New York is tough these days."

Pruhar rushed up. "I was trapped in the cheap seats, but I think you got the better of him. Well, it's not so different from the forty other openings around town tonight. Twenty-five years ago only the critics mugged you. Now it's your fans."

"Come back to my office to sit for a moment," Nora said.

That's when I saw Binny at the door.

In her black leggings and sleeveless peach blouse, I had a good look at her. Her heavy blue sweater gone, I could see she was slender, shapely, not at all flat-chested. You can know everything about a woman's body from the lines of her shoulders. Something about her was fierce, and I wondered suddenly, what could make Binny Sanford cry? Her hair was blacker than I remembered, still spiky. She wore blood-red lipstick and large earrings, two dice.

She smiled when she saw me. I had the same sense I'd had the last time: if I make one wrong move with her, something of immeasurable value will be lost forever.

She took my hand. "Tell me what to look at first," she said. I realized how loud it was in the room; I had to stand close to hear her. I had an unexpected thrill when she spoke into my ear.

It was after nine. A new wave of visitors had filled the gallery, an older, wealthier crowd. Three thousand dollar suits, two hundred dollar ties, handmade loafers, gold, and gemstones. There were conversations in German and French. While Binny looked at Montrose's pictures (she stood completely still, tuned in), she kept her arms behind her back, a posture that thrust her collarbones forward, enlarged the hollows. She breathed quietly. She studied the pictures straight on, not tipping her head like so many viewers. I shivered, but if I had told her of her effect on me she wouldn't have accepted responsibility.

She asked me what Montrose was trying to do. "He thinks of art as a continuous, but badly scarred tradition," I told her. "It's not enough to quote the past he says."

"Where's the past in this one?" she asked. It was a vine image: mossy, vitreous, dense, gorgeous. You could make out two figures locked in struggle.

I told her about composition, about the diamond shape of the *Four Horsemen of the Apocalypse* in Dürer, about the *Raft of the Medusa*.

"It looks like nature fighting itself," she said. "Is that how the vines grew?"

I explained to Binny how Montrose's material came from found forms. The vines did not grow the way they appeared in his prints; it was all imagination reworking the vines we found on our daily excursions into the wilds of New Haven. I explained how I went out and took photos of the vines and how I scanned these photographs (along with pictures from *National Geographic*—Montrose refused to deal with the copyright issues, "Let them come after me," he reasoned) into the computer for him to rearrange and blend. I told her how the ink-jetting was done in Vermont using the disks we sent. I told her that Montrose wanted people to think his wrestling Tree-Men, his Vine-Women, were beautiful.

"You're his apprentice."

"I'm his employee."

"What else do you do for him?"

"Sometimes I have to go out in the dead of night and steal the actual vines from his neighbors' yards."

"Some of them are very beautiful, aren't they?" she said. "He doesn't use much color though."

"I'm trying to teach him."

"Because you're a painter," she said archly.

"Because I know about color."

Binny had large violet eyes. Even in the bright light they dilated.

"Are there any here you don't like?" she asked.

I think she wanted to make sure that I wasn't intimidated by Montrose.

I showed her one where the idea was strong, but the image was badly done.

"Which one is he, your master?" she asked, looking around.

I pointed out Montrose, still red from his exertion, behind the glass in Nora Cengal's office talking to Pruhar and Burr. I didn't bring Binny to meet him because he would meddle. Even in the midst of his show he would want to interrogate her. He would ask where she was from, why she was at the show, what her intentions were toward me.

"Despite your better judgment, you admire him," she said knowingly.

"I'm susceptible," I answered.

✑

As we walked down Madison Avenue, Binny hooked arms with me. I wanted to run into someone I knew; I wanted to be seen with her.

"You feel good," she said.

I have always fallen in love easily.

I didn't know where we were going. Between the florists and the fruit stands, Manhattan was awash in color. Where I grew up, we cut roses and lilacs from bushes that grew on every street and brought nature inside, my mother arranging jelly jars of flowers on the kitchen table to cheer herself. Here the growth came from inside the tiny cluttered stores, and spilled onto the street. Tiny garnet blooms and long-stemmed irises emerged from green pitchers. We passed shelf after shelf of cuttings and dark green leaves, of plums and mangoes, hairy coconuts and bananas. Manhattan was tropical, as humid as Puerto Rico or Vietnam that October night, with a breeze rushing the air. I was sweating, but it felt cleansing after hours in the gallery. Bright lights magnified the sloping displays of kumquats and pomegranates, the fruit of love that Persephone tasted, worth six months in the Underworld. The sidewalks were wet. I wanted to buy something for Binny, bite into it with her.

The steady pressure of her arm and the touch of her palm made me alert.

"I hate those movies where a perfectly reasonable girl dates a jerk," she said, apropos of nothing. I knew she was warning me in a way. I looked down at the dark sidewalk. "But I do like you."

The way she said it was hot music in my ear; it sounded like sex.

"My boyfriend has always been unstable. When we started dating he was persistent. His parents and my parents are old friends. I've known David since we were kids. He loves me very much," she sighed. "I don't know how to get out of it. I can't abandon him."

Boyfriend? I was stunned. Did Binny Sanford prefer her men injured, bleeding from one of her cruel arrows before she took them as lovers? Was she gauging my future grief if I were denied her? Why had she told me his name? I didn't want to know his name, or anything else about him. Didn't she understand that brutal honesty could only produce terrible results? Or was she checking to see if it was my brand of aphrodisiac?

I always liked women to show some anguish. I didn't want them to be completely at peace; I wanted them a little unhappy, to be yearning and a little amoral. I worshiped their weaknesses until I needed to get out, and then I used these weaknesses against them. Binny seemed to want less than Pam had (she'd called me once from Brooklyn after I'd left, but I never called her back) and this was almost a relief. If Binny wanted a triangle, if that's how it had to start with her, I was game.

She pulled in on my arm, moved closer to me as we walked. I couldn't escape without her releasing me. She said nothing more, even as she lifted herself three steps onto the downtown bus. She knew I was confused and unhappy, but she also knew I would get over it.

"You'll call me?" she asked as the doors closed.

∾

After I'd loaded Binny onto her bus, I walked the heart-stinging blocks back to the gallery. I was already sorry that Binny hadn't stayed, although it was obvious she had another date. She had come by just to set a few ground rules and whet my interest.

The crowd had thinned at Cengal. A husband and wife dressed alike in silk with guarded, appraising eyes; a courtly man with perfect posture, alone, in black slacks and a mauve pullover; a single woman in her early forties, recently discarded as a mistress, I imagined, self-absorbed and trying to determine if she believed in love anymore; a small dark-skinned Asian man with a ponytail and his tall, blond, emaciated girlfriend who wore no makeup; a group of women dressed in white pajamas. Nora Cengal was just leaving Montrose's side, taking her place in the center of the gallery. Holding a microphone, she spoke simply and with emotion.

"Tonight it is clear to everybody that my friend Mr. Montrose is not a mirror of the culture but a mirror of the culture to be. For he has made a beautiful art that will be here in fifty years and we are fortunate to have been the first to see it." Nora held up her glass for a toast. In the strong light, her earrings pulsed. The sound of clinking glasses was swallowed in the cavern. "My friend and great patron of the arts, Alex Samon would also like to toast Mr. Montrose."

Samon, whose boots Montrose had complimented not two hours before, came forward from one of the corner couches, his jacket open, his young man's gut starting to show. His hair was gleaming. The studs on his shirt were tiny rubies. At the edges of my vision, his private security force was vigilant. He was under Nora's spell.

Nora handed him the cordless stick. Alex smiled at her. "This city is a wonderful place to me. Mister's pictures are the world to me, the best. I am always happy to buy what Nora Cengal knows is the best." His teeth were too perfect to be real. His accent was heavy with th's. He coughed into the back of his wrist. "Tonight I saw a good fight and a good art."

Nora Cengal stood very still when Mr. Samon hugged her. When his embrace continued a few seconds too long, she made no attempt to move away.

Nora held the microphone out to Montrose who pursed his lips and looked shy, refusing her offer. She carried the microphone over to him and he stood with it.

"I'm not good with one of these things," he said. "But maybe I could get used to it." A few people laughed. "Anyway, you're all here and I'm glad you are. Here's to the Cengal Gallery and the good art that's left in this city." He lifted the microphone skyward like Lady Liberty, then brought it back to his lips. "Does anyone know where the men's room is?" Extending it to Nora, he couldn't resist one final comment and pulled the microphone back, like a coach at a post-game press conference, "Hey, I hope the show held its own." Then he was gone.

I thought of Binny, the contradictory facts of her life—having a long-term boyfriend and coming on to me—and I wanted to call her. Suddenly I was ready to leave New York with her, take her back to my studio and paint a nude. The conditions were such—erotic and personal—that I was prepared. A nude would be my greatest challenge; I was willing to take a chance on heartbreak if she got me working again.

Montrose came back from the men's room.

"Who was that girl?" he asked.

How did he know I was thinking of her? Was I that easy to read? I didn't even know that he had seen Binny. "Which one?"

"Don't try that innocence on me. You know which one," he bellowed. Loud, mock anger was his way of showing affection. "You think I didn't see her? You think I haven't been patient waiting for you to admit to what's going on here?"

"A friend."

"She looked like a nice friend," he said gently, backing off. "Anything more I need to know there?"

"Not right now," I answered.

CHAPTER 5

On the second morning of the trial, Pruhar made himself available to the press in the atrium of the New Haven superior courthouse. Pruhar presented himself to reporters as deeply wounded, but he also clearly enjoyed the spectacle he was at the center of. Once he appeared in *Vanity Fair*, he wanted to be talked about. Pruhar knew the value of publicity as much as he disliked the implications of his portrait in *The Rape of the Muse*. More than once I considered whether his suit against Montrose was less a counterattack than an opportunity for exposure, for marketing himself.

There was no shortage of press in town. On several side streets around the courthouse the networks had parked their giant, antennaed vans. Swinging spotlights allowed for interviews at night. It was unbelievable to me that a dispute about art could generate so much interest among the producers, broadcasters, and the general public. But then, the case had everything—$525-an-hour lawyers, the cult of the artist, a full listing of the price of contemporary artworks, a courtroom-controlled discussion of the proper subjects of art, and a nude woman at the center of a violent act—to fill an early spring media void. Ordinary people had strong opinions about art and The Beautiful it turned out. The man on the street offered his view of the latest blockbuster show he'd attended—Matisse at the Met, Picasso at MoMA. On the morning shows, women spoke of their mosaic and fabric classes. On the evening news, prisoners' advocates promoted the benefits of art therapy. Art therapists defended the work of the insane. Actor Steve Martin's celebrity collection of Impressionist paintings at the Bellagio Hotel in Las Vegas dropped its twelve-dollar entrance fee so that people could come in for free to enjoy art between blackjack hands. Even the perky, usually opinion-less talk show hosts on the morning TV shows spoke of the art in their homes.

At the end of day one, it seemed to me that Montrose was winning his case in only this way: his cybermontage of real bodies and faces had returned the public discussion to artwork that people could describe. Modern art had been impervious to traditional criticism because of its lack of structure, harmony, technique, beauty; this had been one of Montrose's messages. The critic was left to judge the modern artist rather than his work—What was his inner life? Was it distinguished?—and who had the qualifications for that judgment, Montrose wanted to know. Most of the American public seemed to appreciate Montrose's revival of human figures, even if they did not approve of a Rape scene.

Of course, Montrose's motivations, his inner life, were at the center of *Pruhar v. Montrose*. Montrose's friends defended him on the air. Even though every one of them admitted he was "difficult" and competitive, adversarial and opinionated, for twenty years he'd engaged them during visits to Abar Lake or on the phone. They spoke of him as a man of habit, a worker, a model of stability in his home life. When pushed, they admitted he could live the life he did because he had inherited his father's money, his great defense against being pushed to do anything he didn't want to do. But they spoke of his generosity, his purchases of young artists' work, his obvious affection for his wife and daughter. They spoke about his love of art, his stated unwillingness to travel to any place that didn't produce great art. He refused to go to Israel, for instance, or Australia. I had heard the story of Cynthia dragging him to London where he had enjoyed the Tate despite himself. These qualities generated sympathy at the same time he was referred to as a kook and a mad man by Pruhar's allies. On the news, Montrose's face—expressive, imposing, grave, mischievous— became the new millennium's definitive artist's face as it had been the emblem of creativity during America's last war. The national media smothered New Haven. On CNN, I recognized every building, every garden, every brick wall, every cobblestone alley and historic street, every tree root-lifted sidewalk of my town. A television police drama called *New Haven* had been on weekly for three years of Friday nights, so viewers in Oklahoma felt they already knew the city. But now New Haven was everywhere in the news as the new art Mecca, home to famous and volatile sculptors.

ᐧᐧᐧ

Barrow put Pruhar back on the stand. He didn't want to leave the jury with Pontes' cross-examination from the end of the last session.

"Just a few final questions, Mr. Pruhar. Did Mr. Montrose ever mention to you that he had chosen to put you in an allegory?"

"No."

"Did he ever in any way at all say that this picture had some other meaning, some allegorical meaning, and that you shouldn't view it as a rape scene?"

"No."

"Did he ever warn you that he was going to portray you as a rapist?"

"No."

"Or as a dangerous and violent person or as a criminal?"

"No."

"And he's never apologized about his portrayal of you from the time of its publication until now?"

"No."

Barrow walked in a small circle and faced Pruhar again. "These figures are almost life size as reproduced. Mr. Pruhar, for the edification of the court, would you stand next to the picture, Exhibit 1. Please—strike that—can I have you pose next to the picture."

"I thought your client would be incapable of striking a pose," Judge Miller interjected.

"But he is capable of a scowl as in the picture," Barrow said.

"Is it a fact, Mr. Pruhar, that you are capable of a scowl?" Miller asked.

"Yes, I am capable of a scowl."

"I should think so. As you know, that's one of the prerequisites of coming to my court. The Muse looks rather serene," Judge Miller pronounced.

"She looks apprehensive to me," Barrow said

"I don't think she's seen the rapist yet," Miller said.

"She sees his hand sticking out there, it seems to me," Pruhar offered.

"She seems to be looking in the opposite direction, apparently in the direction of the artist," Barrow said. "Mr. Pruhar, would you please stand next to the picture?"

Pruhar started to leave the witness box.

"I don't think that will be necessary," Miller said. "The jury can see both Mr. Pruhar and the picture quite clearly from where they're sitting, I believe."

"I would like to make my one request again," Barrow said. "I would like to have Mr. Pruhar stand before the jury—I'm not going to ask him to put on a trench coat or a mask or a scowl. The jury has seen Mr. Pruhar from the witness stand, but they are entitled to see him next to the picture."

"I am afraid you are going to have an unrequited wish," Miller said. "I don't think they need to see him any more closely than they do already."

"Is there any harm to the defendant?"

"It's not going to happen," Judge Miller said.

"I don't like to argue with the court," Barrow said.

"That's why you're here," Miller said sarcastically.

"I am arguing with Mr. Pontes. I don't want to argue with you. I have one final question for Mr. Pruhar. Do you believe in an allegorical sense that the picture, *The Rape of the Muse*, depicts you as a destroyer of art?"

"But I'm not an allegory. I'm a person," Pruhar said, meaningfully.

⚬℘⚬

In October, Pruhar had picked up several new enthusiasms during his visit to the city for the Cengal show. A visit to New York forced everyone to adjust; back in New Haven, Pruhar told us he had come to believe in female deities. At Montrose's studio, he spoke quickly, in an excited way. "Moon goddess, earth mother, Venus of Mycenae. You know the work. All the muses. Harris, don't you believe in muses?"

I didn't tell him that after seeing Binny Sanford again, I was a believer in muses too. After one weekend in New York, Pruhar believed in magic, in luck, in coincidence, in private time to develop his "spiritual health." On the advice of an organic healer he'd met in his hotel's lobby, he planned to bathe regularly in rock salt and look for silver in his urine.

"Don't start that shit on me," Montrose said, looking up from his computer screen. Across the road, Abar Lake was stupendous in the autumn afternoon sunlight. Yellow and red leaves floated on its shiny silver surface. A family of water birds landed along the far shore. Montrose gently lifted Jake and Scout off the work table where they were rubbing against the tiny pedestal he was repairing.

Pruhar ingeniously disguised his excitement as investigative scholarship. He said he was bowing to the moon nine times a day now and reading complicated texts. He drew from his breast pocket pictures of ancient Goddesses that Montrose wouldn't look at, but I was eager to consider. I knew that Pruhar only half-believed what he reported. His eyes twinkled. I knew he was not suddenly an innocent New Ager. He had probably seen a crystal he'd been aesthetically drawn to and let himself get carried away. I was used to seeing him upbeat,

89

high voltage, a man interested in everything, a man who could be easily distracted because his mind was already racing.

"Muses," Montrose smirked, "is that your new way in?"

Pruhar stood behind Montrose, looking at the computer screen.

"What do you think of this one?" Montrose asked him, clicking a new image onto the screen.

"I like that one," Pruhar said, coming around the table. His teeth were perfect and bright. "I'll make T-shirts from it. You'll get eight percent."

"Is that a good deal?" Montrose asked.

"That's what Calvin Klein gets on accessories he licenses." Pruhar was up on modern commerce. Where did he get his information?

"Fame is not a lottery," Pruhar mocked. "You can't just be working in your studio. You have to be out there presenting your work. The Goddesses can help." He badly wanted Montrose to accept his Goddesses.

"So what's the other news you wanted to tell me?" Montrose asked Pruhar.

"I'm getting a new studio. I'm moving from City Point to West River. More space."

"What do you need a new studio for?"

"New work."

"You have the money for it?"

I remembered that Cynthia had recently said to me, "My husband loves Simon. He's family. Harris lays awake thinking how he can explain to Simon that he needs to protect his money, not throw it away. He wants to protect Simon from himself."

"I think so," Pruhar said.

"Well, then you're okay."

Just that morning I'd heard Montrose speak on the phone with an old friend, a marble carver, Ed Giancini, who'd just bought his first house at age forty. Montrose praised his friend for becoming a property owner while warning him about the vagaries of real estate, the backwardness of thinking of one's house as an investment. Montrose liked solid practicality. (During my initial interview he wanted to know what kind of television I owned). I knew Montrose had lent Giancini money for the house so he could have a studio rather than having to work in the living room among his five children. Montrose was generous to his artist friends; he admired Ed's ambition to work in marble even though he thought the pieces were failures so far.

"What kind of work do you need a new studio for?" Montrose wanted to know.

"Actually, I need the space for new pottery work."

"Look what you're wearing!" Montrose yelled.

"It's jade," Pruhar said. A sickle-shaped piece the size of a child's smile hung from a black cord around his neck.

"I know it's jade," Montrose said. "But why?"

"Look at this shade of green."

"Don't people laugh at you when they see it? A grown man wearing a little rock like that? It's terrible. It's just awful. Promise me you'll stop doing that. No more." He didn't say it in a mean or abusive tone, but matter-of-factly.

I loved Pruhar's pieces. On his invitation, I'd been over to his workshop to have a closer look. His pottery was sculptural and delicate: pillboxes with tiny strata of platinum, tea services decorated with irregular, organic beads, celadon-glazed salt and pepper shakers set in gold feet. He avoided silver, which he viewed as too undependable, weak, cheap. Pruhar came back again and again to Abar Lake with his designs for low cups and sugar bowls, hoping each time that Montrose might approve of his newest project. But Montrose was impossible to impress.

"I'm going to be making a line of tea and coffee sets for Nieman Marcus," Pruhar said.

No wonder he knew Calvin Klein's commission percentage. He'd been in negotiations himself and had done some homework.

"I didn't know Nieman Marcus sold ceramics," I said.

91

"It doesn't. Not yet. That's what this sabbatical I'm taking is for," Pruhar said. "To make some new designs, manufacture them, see if I can really interest them."

Behind us, the door opened and Cynthia walked in. I didn't know she was home. She had been away for almost three weeks, but her mother was now back in Jacksonville, fully recovered from pneumonia.

"You haven't moved this big box out of here yet," she said, exasperated. She was wearing a gray sweater, jeans, and black shoes with low heels. She didn't look like the CEO of a financial consulting firm. Montrose told me Fleet Bank was interested in buying her out.

"Thank God you're here," Montrose called out. "You're not going to believe what Simon's done."

"What now?" Cynthia teased.

"He's trying to go into the cup and bowl business."

"He's been making ceramics for years," Cynthia said.

"No, this is very bad. I'm not making myself clear."

"Harris, stop it," she said.

"I'm not allowed to talk to you about this now," he said to Pruhar, as if he always listened to his wife's instructions.

Pruhar removed from his pocket a sphere of gauze the size of a ping-pong ball. Inside was a miniature crimson teapot, a wheel-thrown porcelain the size of a thimble. He removed its micro lid and laid it on the desk. Cynthia nodded appreciatively. With hardly a glance, Montrose criticized it for artistic laziness.

Why was Montrose so bothered by Pruhar's ceramics-making? What I had seen in my earliest days at Abar Lake as a low-level disparagement of Pruhar's move from sculpture toward ceramics had, in the past month, beginning with his attack in front of Molly Vidian, turned more vicious. Did Montrose believe that seeking Nieman Marcus' approval (it was impressive to me that Pruhar had even penetrated the upscale retailer's organization) was more about ego gratification than about serious work and the creative spirit? Was it that ceramics was so purely "about career" as he'd said to Vidian? Did he believe that Pruhar shouldn't get special consideration for creating a line of breakfast sets for Nieman, the embodiment of high-priced New York commercialism? Was he jealous of Pruhar's action? Before Cengal, Montrose had claimed he wanted no public attention; if he didn't want any, Pruhar shouldn't either.

Or was Montrose simply angry at the world because not a single New York critic had reviewed his Cengal show? Being ignored must have caused him pain, but he kept it hidden. Perhaps Montrose feared Pruhar would fail too, and he wanted to protect his old friend from grief.

∞

I'd called Schuyler for advice about Binny's surprise visit at the Cengal opening, and without warning, he'd bought a ticket to visit me. He appeared at my door the day after I got back to New Haven, where the October weather had suddenly turned chilly. I was shocked to see him in Connecticut. The circles under his eyes were darker than usual, and his beard, which never really filled in, looked scruffy. Schuyler went up and down ten pounds in a week depending on what he ate, but he seemed particularly thin, his belt loose.

"You sounded down last night when you called," he said. "I thought I'd let you take me out for lunch. I figured you weren't coming back to New York again soon, and I couldn't sleep anyway. I took the six AM Bonanza Express out of Port Authority."

"Aren't you working today?" I asked. Tuesdays I painted in my studio, with my cat Occo, front paws decorously crossed, watching from the counter next to the sink. A mile and a half west of Abar Lake, it was a day away from Montrose. The truth was I didn't want to be interrupted, even by Schuyler. I thought I'd made a good start on a new canvas for the first time in three months and was eager to get back to it.

"I needed to get out of the city. Be in the woods. You have woods around here, right?"

"Are things with Madeline okay?"

"There were other people I didn't mind getting away from for a day."

I thought he meant another woman. Schuyler played around. He attracted women of all types, from thick-legged department store makeup countergirls to wealthy, tanned widows trying to rediscover their youth.

After the unusual warm spell of the previous weeks, Canadian weather had arrived. The few pedestrians looked red-faced and swollen. Schuyler had picked up a paper at the bus station to point out for me the weaknesses of my fellow New Havenites. Most of the people in the state seemed to be trying to get themselves bad names, he reported. Credit unions were going under, there were felons in City Hall. Two FBI stings of the mayor's office had produced three more indictments. Four ounces of cocaine had mysteriously disappeared inside police headquarters. The former governor, recently released from prison, was trying to reclaim his pension. The Health Department had announced that, per capita, the state had the most smokers, the most sedentary workforce, and the highest cancer rate in the country. The new furniture store, large enough to block the view of downtown from the highway, had to hire twenty-four-hour protection for the sheetrock that was going in; even the cheapest building supplies were being vandalized in my new hometown. Schuyler enjoyed reading every headline to me.

At eleven AM, he was ready for lunch. He rarely ate lunch, a habit left over from his boxing days when he had to make weight. He must have missed his usual egg and pancake breakfast because of the early bus ride.

Schuyler had boxed at 138 pounds, training in Mount Vernon where his family lived. Schuyler called boxing "the most psychologically useful preparation for painting." At school, he was out to attack his rivals and was quick to see a slight. He believed in aggression not apology, passion not sympathy. He never gossiped with me about classmates. Gossiping was not for the self-righteous, and Schuyler felt he was always right; he occupied the high ground. He accused *me* of being impudent. I had often heard him quote my line—"There are only two acceptable reactions to art, awe or hate"—but he was the one who was known as arrogant, with his mannerism of holding his cigarette between the third and fourth fingers.

"Let's go next door, you can buy me a hamburger if you want more advice on your dream woman," Schuyler said.

We went into McGilray's down the street. We sat at the bar where they served double-salted peanuts from a bamboo bowl. The mirror was too small and crowded with the reflections of bottles. My father used to buy a bottle of Smirnoff every few years, empty it into an unmarked bottle he kept in his den, and refill the Smirnoff liter with cheaper vodka he brought out to offer visitors. I wondered how many of the bottles in front of me actually contained what they said they did.

"My father thought beer couldn't make you drunk if you had it with ice," Schuyler said.

Behind us, fat local businessmen, CPAs with poor color, and suit salesmen from Silver J Clothing were already eating buffalo chicken wings with blue cheese dip and chewing ginger ale-soaked ice cubes, their jackets on the backs of their chairs. Suspenders were everywhere and looked ridiculous, I thought, a sign of poor self-esteem, a last-ditch effort at fashion.

"Did Montrose sell anything?" Schuyler asked, bored with the subject of my love life before we'd even begun. He wanted to know numbers; he wanted to know prices. He followed the art market closely; on his desk at work was a pile of glossy catalogs from Christie's and Sotheby's. He had calculated Montrose's worth six times for me since I'd moved, estimating the value of Montrose's house based on my description of the lake view and recent neighborhood house sales he found on the Internet. Schuyler had asked me more than once how many credit cards Montrose had and how quickly he paid his bills, questions I couldn't answer. I'd never seen Schuyler write a check and wondered whether he even had a bank account. Schuyler was envious of Montrose's wealth, the People's United bank account filled with the inheritance from his father's bottled water business; he speculated that dividends streamed into Montrose's pocket.

"I think he sold three," I said. I didn't add what a disappointment this had been.

"How was the circle of old-timers, old Burr? Adoring, disgruntled, nostalgic, or embittered?"

Schuyler and Burr never hit it off. He thought Burr's albino hands were creepy. He thought Burr was a perfectionist and a downer. Burr demanded impossible results from himself and his students; as a teacher he was bound to be disappointed. He had attacked Schuyler's work ethic once too often.

"You never know with Burr."

"So this marvelous, beautiful woman you've met," Schuyler began. He always gave me bad advice about women, but with authority, and I always came back for more. He was, after all, an expert. I knew his approach. In the beginning, courting, Schuyler spent the money he had. He bought drinks, flowers, books, antique fountain pens. If he was serious, he would give women sable paintbrushes with soft, thick white bristles, or sketchbooks with heavy paper. Slowly, Schuyler's charm replaced his gifts, and after an expensive dinner, he would display the thinnest square of leather—his wallet—the new lover had ever seen. Its flatness broke her heart. He only dated women with steady incomes, and once they'd seen this wallet they began paying. They bought him extravagant presents: mountain bikes, tiny gold Buddhas, stacks of scented candles. He was an artist who looked like an innocent, who offered hand-rolled clove cigarettes to the ones who secretly wanted to smoke again. His poverty was endearing; spending his last artistic dollars on them was a sign of true love. "I wouldn't invite her to New Haven. Why let a woman who lives in New York ruin your life? Didn't you already do that? But that doesn't seem to matter to you. Remember Pam? She's still in Brooklyn pining for you. You should really move back to the city."

Schuyler had a fondness for Pam Knightsley, the woman I'd dated just before moving to New Haven. Pam was a graduate student in mathematics at NYU whose field was imaginary numbers. She was trustworthy and had the most delicate cough, dry and childlike. She wore socks to bed, but undressed she was not as shy as I expected given her line of study and her wide awkward feet. Sex with Pam was slow and drowsy, her long straight hair on me, her sharp elbows nudging me into angles she enjoyed. I would run my nails down her back, and she would touch the tip of my penis with her knees trying to revive me. She had wonderful legs. When I first met her she wore black stockings with musical notations on them, tiny clefs and quarter notes. Still, she was conventional in most ways, except for her hair, which she had not cut in fifteen years. It covered her rear end, and at the gallery openings I'd hear people ask, "Who is the woman with the hair?" It was the desired effect.

Pam never wore bras, preferring slips and shifts and camisoles. Her rooms were all white, sparsely furnished and cool. She had a beautiful hourglass of a body and skinny ankles. Obsessed with her body, its pleasures and distresses, she would talk endlessly about her ice-pick headaches and menstrual cramps. She used baby powder, perhaps thinking of the baby she desperately wanted, and I had no trouble imagining one filling her wide hips.

In her female mind, I was an equation to solve, I suppose. I think when she realized that unlike many men, I didn't really need to be in a couple—I cooked, I sewed, I preferred time alone—she felt challenged. I thought as much about painting as Pam did about numbers, day and night. Even when I was chosen by the *Times*, she could still not get herself to believe that I didn't mind being by myself, painting; she got stuck on the sad untruth she imagined. From early on, she kept asking me to clarify my intentions, which I really couldn't do for her because I had no intentions.

I could not have moved to New Haven so easily if Pam and I hadn't fought over my painting, or lack of it. She suggested that maybe I needed a break from painting. Infuriated, I suggested that maybe I needed a break from her. We split up three or four times during my last month in the city, and always in the same way. I called her a hypochondriac, she loathed me, spent a few days forgiving me, then called again. I kept picking fights with her to make a point; she would ask to come over and we would sleep together.

I had not been unhappy, finally leaving her. She wanted me to stay so she could change my life, make me a different person. Her complaints were always logical, mathematical in their simplicity. She seemed in perfect control of herself until she lost it one Monday, when she started crying and shaking abjectly.

"Pam wanted you in New York, so you moved to Connecticut to concentrate on your work," Schuyler said. "Now I get the feeling you're concentrating on Montrose's work rather than your own, and getting involved with a Binny from Manhattan as an added distraction." How did he know I still wasn't painting much; he'd only glanced into my studio from the door. "You're a flake. On the other hand, if you start coming back to town regularly, I'll be glad to have you back."

I knew Schuyler felt I'd deserted him, but couldn't say it. For whatever reason, he would not encourage me to call Binny, and I could feel myself backing even further away from phoning her. Then a vision of her went through my head: the pale freckles on her upper chest and forearms.

"There are complications with Binny," I said.

"Already?"

"Why not? Aren't there always complications? Better to deal with them early on."

"Is this what you learned from Pam?" Schuyler asked me. "There weren't complications with *her* early on. She just wanted to marry you. She was clear right off. You're trying to get someone as different from Pam as possible? Someone a little muddy?"

Schuyler had always defended Pam. Pam who liked exposed brick. Pam who trained me to ask about her day. Pam who felt I should make a commitment to regular mealtimes.

"Pam was not unreasonable. She wanted reasonable things. She wanted a middle class life. You're the one who made her think she could have one with you," Schuyler reminded me.

"You're one to talk about settling down," I said.

"I would have considered it if she had asked *me*."

"She's available," I said.

"Is Binny?" he asked.

"Binny doesn't have those needs. She's not like that." I spoke as though I knew something about her.

"So tell me what she's like, Binny. What are Binny's needs?" he asked mockingly.

I told him again about my unforgettable first glimpse of her, my instant infatuation, her ready interest in me.

"She has another boyfriend." I swallowed the words with my McGilray's chowder.

"Go on." He didn't seem surprised.

"But she seems to want me in the mix too."

"Well, that's one approach. A woman who knows what she wants and isn't afraid to ask. She wants the two of you to meet, I presume," he said snidely. Schuyler had a repertoire of smiles that spanned disdain to amusement. When he laughed hard he would start to cough, a smoker's hack.

"So you're willing to put up with this woman's bullshit," Schuyler continued. He picked at his club sandwich, wouldn't eat the crust, pulled out the bacon. He drank dark ale and smoked half a cigarette before lighting up the next one. "Undisguised, right up front she tells you, informs you, that there will be someone else around. Or rather, she *won't* be around because she'll be with someone else."

"I'm here, she's there. We'll see where it goes," I said. "It means I don't have to be serious. I can just have some fun."

"You don't know how to have fun."

"I've started some new work with her in it." I'd barely begun, but I was thinking about Binny every minute of the day. Art was about pauses and renewal to Schuyler, about complaining and boasting, and he wouldn't have been sympathetic to my problems if I'd told him. He didn't feel bad when he wasn't working; he'd given himself a permanent not-guilty verdict. He expected daily, fearless output from me; I was his model of steadiness and consistency. "I've got plenty of pictures in my head," he used to say during his downturns. "I'm just not sure whether I want to give them a second look."

"That's just libido," he said, puffing hard. "You're an asshole. But an optimistic asshole. What does she do for work?"

"She's a music critic."

"So she's always falling in love, or out of it," Schuyler said. I was lost.

"Critics are always in love or just over it," he explained. "By definition. They have intense curiosity and a jaded palate."

Sometimes I thought Schuyler's talk was better than his painting, an exercise in what I once heard called, "the athletics of personality."

"If you're asking my advice: it doesn't sound good to me. But go ahead. Enjoy the torture," he said. "I am actually interested in meeting her now."

"She's coming up here next weekend." I couldn't wait to see her. I thought of the slow up and down of her hips when she walked.

"New Haven is part of the Red Sox nation, isn't it?" Schuyler asked, fed up with Binny talk. On these raw days he was already looking forward to spring.

"Seattle Mariners nation actually," I said. "We have the Ravens, the Double-A farm team, playing right in town."

"The whole place is minor league," Schuyler said. He was a tireless Yankees fan. He'd once dated a pharmaceutical saleswoman to take advantage of her third baseline seats in the

Bronx. "Including Montrose." He couldn't stop himself from the jab. "New York is keener, more demanding, the stimulations are more rewarding; so are the women.

"Say, who paid for that fancy hotel you were staying at this weekend?" The Tuscany's front desk had a basket of red pears; I grabbed one every trip in and out so I wouldn't have to buy the twelve-dollar coffee shop burgers.

"You know who paid," I answered.

"Who's paying for that apartment you're staying in?" I teased back, knowing it was Madeline.

"You may think there's some lesson you can learn from Montrose's career," Schuyler said for the twentieth time, "but there isn't."

When we got back to my apartment, Schuyler decided to inspect my new work. From two evenings with her, I'd started a picture of Binny, her wide mouth and thin eyebrows. I figured her upcoming visit meant she would stay with me, she would sleep with me, she would pose nude and I'd paint her perfect skin, her beautiful throat and belly. When Schuyler saw the start of this picture, he picked up the phone. "Let's call this Binny," he said. "See what she's about. See what she's doing on a perfectly ordinary day like today."

"You can't call her," I said.

"Of course, I can. I'm not the one who wants to make an impression."

"You can't just check her out like that. She'll think I put you up to it."

"Didn't you? Isn't that why you asked my advice? I can't give advice, sight unseen, voice unheard. I need to get a feel for her, excuse the pun."

It felt a little mean unleashing Schuyler on her, but it was also potentially funny. See if Binny Sanford had a sense of humor. Any insight into Binny would help. And didn't she deserve a little cruelty coming back at her?

"Don't tell her I'm with you," I warned him.

"Of course not."

"She's probably home," I told him, reciting the number. "She does her work at night."

"I know and *you* know that you don't know where she is right now. Yes, I know you want to tell me there's no *reason* you should know her whereabouts, she doesn't owe you that. But listen to me: you lose a little and then you lose a little more to a woman like this. Once the arrangement you're establishing is in place, there's no going back. You should set some rules in these first weeks.

"Is this Elizabeth Sanford, also known as Binny?" Schuyler said into the receiver. "This is Arden Schuyler, a friend of Rand's. Well, we're actually here together in New Haven." He winked at me before I could get angry. "We were talking about you over lunch and Rand wanted to call." Here Binny said something I couldn't hear although Schuyler held the receiver up in the air for me. "I'm speaking with you because I wanted to call also. He'll talk with you next. He was a little uncertain so I wanted to clarify your plans with him." Binny said something more as Schuyler giggled. "You don't have a plan?" Here Schuyler winked at me. "Well, not consciously maybe," he said to her. "Anyway, I wanted to make sure you understood that Rand likes the most banal art. He can't help himself."

"Loyal friends. That's a good sign," Binny said to me when I wrestled the phone away from Schuyler. "He's affectionate, but he turns on people, holds grudges, but never without cause."

"You got that right," I answered, stunned a little by her insight.

"Well, he checked me out," she said. "Tell me how I did when I see you."

⌒

Anyone who picked up the *New Haven Register* on the second day of the trial saw a picture of Montrose that was a gem. Montrose looked like a saint, his eyes cast up, his hands groping toward the camera, lips slightly parted. It made him oddly sympathetic. By a trick of perspective, he looked tiny. So small, what chance did he have?

I'd watched the reporters pursue him on his way out of superior court at the lunch break. I was across the street when I heard the stampede of feet running toward him as he walked with Cynthia down Church Street toward their car. I started to move forward to protect him.

"Can we talk to you for a minute, Mr. Montrose?"

He ignored the journalists on his heels. The few people outside the courthouse turned to stare at the bearish man with the long, flying gray hair, and moved out of the way of the group of twenty pursuers. Montrose had become an important piece of gossip. Because he'd once held himself aloof, now he was an especially valuable media target, available for scorn. The European and New York paparazzi on his tail regarded any attempt at escape as an insult. The artist who had hidden for twenty-five years had produced a nude centerfold for *Vanity Fair*.

And the nude was Binny, posing in a photograph she'd sent me and that I'd shown Montrose in a moment of pride, and which he'd appropriated, promising to make her unidentifiable. She and I hadn't spoken since the picture appeared.

From her attendance at the trial, I presumed Barrow had been in touch with her and was planning to put her on the stand. Seeing her in court, a surge of expectation had risen in me, but did not get very far. She'd come to the trial but managed to avoid me. She was still angry; she believed that I had told Montrose to put her in his picture, or at least allowed it. She was wrong, but I hadn't convinced her. A kind of illumination had settled on her skin in the months since I'd seen her. Her beauty had deepened. I wondered if the press was chasing her as hard as they were chasing Montrose.

At the corner of Elm and Temple, across from the public library, a photographer jumped out from behind a car, barring Montrose's way. "Hold it," she said.

Montrose averted his face as a flash went off in the shadow of an elm.

"Can we speak?" she asked. She had an accent—Spanish, Italian. Her press credentials hung from a chain around her neck.

"What about?" Montrose asked mock-innocently.

A tape recorder appeared in her hand, thrust at his midsection. He pushed it away.

"About why you did it."

"Did what?"

The camera flashed again. Cynthia, who disliked being photographed, edged a step away from Montrose, still holding his hand.

"You know, the rape scene."

"Now, even you know that I can't comment on that. You can hear me tomorrow."

"Okay. So what can you comment on?"

"The artistic principles at stake here."

The other reporters had now gathered around, and I had crept up behind them so that I could see him the way they did.

On this warm May day on a New Haven street corner, Montrose held forth. He couldn't help it. He didn't try to charm or manipulate. For a minute or two, he spoke in a serious and genuine way about beauty and the freedom necessary to make it.

"Are you a workaholic?" a reporter interrupted.

"I hate that word, workaholic. I hate when I'm told that working is just an excuse for being anti-social. 'Isn't it terrible that people work so much?'" Montrose mimicked. "People who get to the point where their work is satisfying are lucky people."

"Are you sorry?" a woman in a blue peacoat asked. "Do you regret what you did?"

Montrose paused. He suddenly understood that his audience didn't care about art. "Not at all."

"So you'd do it again?"

"I have no interest in repeating myself."

A camera clicked from above. A photographer had climbed a nearby tree.

The reporter smiled. She wanted more. She had pages to fill. She wanted a story, which meant she wanted him to be indiscreet.

"Come on, can somebody ask me a real question," Montrose said.

At that moment I realized, despite all his denials, Montrose wanted to be known. He had put in his time, produced an enormous amount of work and he wanted his work recognized, quoted, sought-after. He wanted to be known as a distinguished artist, a Giacometti or Rodin, and if he had to teach a group of uncaring journalists about great art, he would.

"Why don't you apologize to Mr. Pruhar?"

"I'm the one getting sued. Don't you think he should apologize to me?" He had turned on his Southern accent. Like Pruhar, he was presenting himself as the victim, the boy from New Orleans. Cynthia couldn't stand it anymore and pulled him away.

CHAPTER 6

The Saturday after she spoke to Schuyler on the phone in my apartment, when the end-of-October leaves were making their way from green to brown via yellow, orange and red, Binny made it to New Haven from New York in just over an hour in her Jetta. Her father, it turned out, was the famous Porsche Spider racer Park Sanford. In the 1970's, no less than J. C. Petty said Park Sanford walked on water. Park's sons had stayed out of the racing business, but his daughter had caught the bug. On weekends as a teenager, Binny raced at small tracks across New Jersey and learned how to take down and rebuild a car. You heard the old pit crew boss in her voice; she had her father's toughness and vulgarity. An hour was damn fast though. I knew the stretch of route 95 she'd driven; my friends and I used to drink and shoot the tollbooths at midnight at seventy miles per hour, no room for error.

God, it was good to see her. When I opened the door of my apartment she was wearing a black sleeveless blouse. She had three small gold earrings in her left ear, none in her right, which I noticed for the first time had a split lobe, an attractive defect. But it was the silver ring on her left thumb that got to me. Thumb rings excited me, I'm not sure why. It was as if the woman wearing the ring belonged to a special tribe and would teach me secret rituals. Sharp blonde hairs grew in Binny's armpits, which I could feel when she hugged me. She'd been eating a Drake's coffee cake and I wanted to brush the crumbs away from her top lip.

Occo came in, winding between her legs, a good omen.

"I was just talking to a friend on the phone about you," I said. Binny didn't ask what I'd been saying. Why not? I wondered. Surely she wanted to know. How was it possible not to ask; I would have. She had miraculous self-control.

"Schuyler?"

"Actually, no," I lied, not wanting to seem predictable.

"A man with two friends, how odd. Do you have many friends?"

"A few," I answered.

"Men don't work at their friendships, which is why they don't usually have many," she said.

I told her how, that week, I'd left three messages for Schuyler at the museum, but he'd never gotten back to me and I refused to call him a fourth time. I was annoyed.

"Oh, just call him again," Binny suggested, throwing her small black nylon bag on the floor.

"I'm done. I've called him plenty."

"But you want to talk to him. So call again," she said.

"No. I don't think so."

"Why not? Pride?"

Montrose understood when I complained about Schuyler. I'd told him about Schuyler taunting me with an unnamed New York curator who, he reported, had been asking him about my painting for a show in December. "You want me to have a word with your friend for you?" Montrose offered. "I wouldn't call him again if I were you."

Binny took the opposite approach in her advice about Schuyler: she tried to shame me into calling. I'd known Binny for barely two months. We'd been at an art lecture together and the Cengal opening, and I'd walked her to one bus; I'd spoken to her on the phone four or five times. Here she was, in my apartment, challenging me. I was still worried that she would leave me as quickly as she had found me.

She wanted a tour. To the left of the front door was an alcove with enough room for a futon mattress and a low table that held a reading lamp shaped like a dove. I slept in this loft overlooking the workspace, a wooden rail protecting me from a twenty-foot drop. Below, down the stairs to the right of the door, was a kitchen area, a small bathroom, and a large cube of studio space. In the late afternoon sun, the room constantly shifted colors—gold, ochre, amber, deep gray, puffs of silver green.

She wanted to see my paintings. We went downstairs to the studio where the oversized hammock, still up from my siesta, split the work area.

"So you're having some trouble getting started in New Haven, I see," she said, flipping through a pile of nearly blank canvases leaning against a wall. Her blouse was untucked, the top and bottom buttons open. In profile, she had perfect, short eyelashes.

"Well, here's a start." She'd found the female torso I'd begun in the days after meeting her.

"You're preparing for a breakthrough, I can tell," she said. "Why don't you paint me?"

I didn't answer her. Did she also have a nude in mind? I hadn't told her the canvas I'd started *was* her. I wanted to ask her to undress. I wanted to start and finish the painting and make love for every minute in between, but in a little over an hour we were due at Pruhar's fiftieth birthday party in Clinton, sixty miles north. Also, I didn't want to seem too eager.

"I know we don't have time to paint right now. Let's take a walk before we get in the car," she suggested. She wanted me to show her how downtown New Haven had changed in the years since her last visit. On Greene Street, Binny walked fast, turned and walked backward when I fell behind. I asked her questions about music and her family. She spoke in long, up-tempo sentences about her father—who had studied mechanical engineering before moving over to car racing—and whose idea of a treat was to take the family to McDonald's for breakfast.

Raised around three brothers, she told me she didn't accept that she was different from boys until her period started one day when she was hanging upside down on the neighborhood jungle gym. She was a tomboy. Her brothers used to tease and slug her and talk sports. She asked me about the Red Sox and their rivalry with the Yankees. I wondered if she was drawing an analogy about me and the other man, my counterpart in New York. The Sox, heroic losers; the Yankees, historic and remarkable. I was jealous of every other man who'd ever met her.

"It's taken me a few months, but I'm beginning to like New Haven," I said. "You have to appreciate it in very particular ways: Don't think of it as a big city. Don't think of it as a place to make a fortune. Think of it as a suburb of Manhattan. Think of it as a place where you can get your work done. In Connecticut, no one is trying to make a name outside of Connecticut. The world ends at the borders with New York and Massachusetts."

Growing up in New Haven would have deeply affected me, I thought. Believing everything was safer and cleaner and superior to your home city, listening to the evening news and hearing about all the urban disasters—the water main breaks, the arsons, the school closings—must have had lasting effects on a child's sense of the world. Despite my new home's famous university, there had recently been an article in *Connecticut Monthly* suggesting Hartford should annex New Haven. The mayor went on TV to defend against a hostile takeover, while the New York media had a good laugh that anyone would have taken the article seriously.

Binny laughed about my home and started to talk again about autistic, five-year-old Timmy, the nephew she visited often at her sister's in Albany. "When he's in a good mood he follows me around. He learned to kiss last week. He kisses me all day. He has this playhouse in the room. I fling open the shutters—'I see you'—and he kisses me. We shoot baskets with a Nerf ball—I do, then he copies. And he kisses me after each shot. When he gets overexcited he gets frustrated. He starts to bite. He bit me last week. It hurt. He drew blood, I have the bruise." She showed me the back of the left forearm where she had obviously attempted to block his attack. "That really pissed me off. But he doesn't know. I tried to show him the wound, but I don't know if he got it."

She spoke about him fondly as we passed the Pro-Pain theatre and Down City Diner and a Charles Schwab outlet. I was moved by her engagement with her nephew, her close observation. Child development was beyond me. Everyone under sixteen years old seemed unyielding and shrill. But Binny was sweetly protective of her sister's son, surprisingly gentle considering her brutal judgment of bands.

"I need to have some fun at this party you're dragging me to," she said in her mock-serious tone as I handed her the keys and we climbed into my truck. I wanted to see Park Sanford's daughter in action behind the wheel.

Binny drove fast and accepted any space opened to her. At ninety MPH, she wanted to talk about success. She had hung around race car drivers her whole life and had opinions about greatness. She believed that if you thought well of yourself, you'd win. Racers valued talent, she told me, but less than they appreciated self-confidence. Binny did not believe in firm natural limitations; it was why she liked Bob Dylan's voice; why, as a seventeen-year-old shoe-horned into a silver, fire-resistant jumpsuit, she drove the track against the clock as her father had. "I have to believe the decision to be a great painter, like being a great racer, is to swim in the essence of self," she said. She was trying to inspire me, but who spoke like that—"the essence of self"? Driving, she was happily erotic, magically erotic, definitively erotic.

Small and rural, Clinton, an oceanside village of eighteenth- and ninetheenth-century houses, was not in any tourist guide. I'd been there once before, dropping off some pictures for Montrose. We passed farmers selling the season's last potatoes, cabbage, and kale at roadside stands. We passed unsteady barns and boarded-up soft ice cream stands. We were headed down the peninsula, and unmarked roads running to the left and right led to multimillion-dollar shore estates. When we reached the bait shops, we started to see the bay through the trees. In the late afternoon, above the pines, long cloud lines of red ran upward like fingernail marks on a pale back of sky. I saw why Pruhar said it was his favorite place in the world. The world of birdbaths and daylilies, screen doors and scraped dishes, and well-fed Labrador retrievers. Newport, Rhode Island, eight nautical miles east, was the summer playground of tourists with its all-night regatta bars; Clinton's cottages shut down at eight PM. There was nothing for tourists to do here, no trinket shops, and you had to pay to get on the beaches. There was also no art community; Pruhar had to import it if he wanted one.

Binny honked at a Cadillac that kept braking for no reason, and gave me her ideas about car horns. She thought they needed updating. She felt they should be expressive, not single-note noisemakers. Each driver needed a repertoire of sounds. One that signaled impatience, another anger, another thanks, another disdain, and so on. Perhaps even one for happiness. Binny wanted a scale of notes that would express personality as well as send an immediate message. People spent so much time in cars, had such intensely good and bad times in them, she believed this would be liberating. She would not accept my suggestion that horns should actually speak. Music was enough for her, the road should be musical.

The Pruhars' house was on Main Road, hidden behind pines and a hedge of honeysuckle. The driveway, a forty-yard path of crushed clam shells, was marked for the occasion by bouquets of balloons. Hearing the crunch of mollusks beneath us and feeling the cover of century-old trees overhead was calming for me. Rabbits sprinted across the grass.

The house was on the right, a rectangle of grass to the left where cars were parking side by side, front ends touching a low stone wall beyond which were dark woods. It was dusk and the white shells lit the way. It was a beautiful piece of land, and Binny stepped out into the cool evening air moving with an easy magic. She headed toward a bed of wildflowers beside the barn, where inside a band was playing. "In New York, I miss the sound of insects," she said. The grass was softened further by pine needles. The main house was three stories of gray clapboard, not a little cottage. It had a steep roof with dormers from which you'd have a view of the water. On the porch sat a basin filled with ice and bottles and cans. Beyond the house was a pond and I could hear the rustling of marsh grass.

Inside, there were prominent artists from Boston and jewelry makers from Rhode Island who mixed with realtors and radio producers and academics. I was uncomfortable talking to my New York friends about my job with Montrose. But at this party plenty of people knew Montrose, admired him, and didn't see me as a traitor for being his assistant. I could smell the ocean, and I thought of my father and a motorboat he'd once piloted for me on Lake Champlain. A windless day, orange peels and Budweiser cans floating by. I felt trapped on the boat, restless, hungry. Straddling the boat and the dock, I'd accidentally dropped my lunch into the water before we'd left shore.

I wondered how many people Pruhar had invited from New York. "The earth curves toward Fifty-Seventh Street," Pruhar would often say. I suddenly felt unbalanced; I hadn't done enough work and stood among artists who had.

I whispered these feelings to Binny who said, brightly, "They're thirty years older than you are." She envied no one, an anomaly at a party where everyone envied someone. Having arrived with Binny, a few eyes envied me. Her short red skirt revealed beautiful knees. She smelled of new mown hay. She had been invigorated by her drive; on the race track I knew she'd been murderous.

But her comment only made me panicky—what if I got to be their age and had nothing to show? I could have done without the party, but Pruhar had been very disturbed turning fifty and I wanted to lend my support. Also, I wanted to show off Binny.

The room was filled with handcrafted wooden furniture and modern ceramics. There were ancients spears, and Persian textiles, and some of Pruhar's older work, a bent and flowing girder beam assemblage. One windowsill held a row of low candles, another a set of flawless crystal snakes.

I was a sucker for buffets, although I was sure to overeat. I couldn't stop when food was lined up like that, when I could carry away two or three plates. I was destined to repeat the circuit until I became bloated, until I had to loosen my belt. I had no sense of restraint. This buffet had a southern theme—fried okra, chicken-fried steak, Vidalia onions, fried shrimp, coleslaw—a remembrance of Pruhar's art school years in New Orleans, in the days before he went, at age twenty-four, to New York; when he got in to see Joseph Hirshhorn who was about to construct a little museum in Washington, D.C. These were the days when Pruhar convinced Hirshhorn—the rich man's appetite voracious for large bronzes—to buy a *Pruhar* bronze. The first of Pruhar's great coups. His first taste of fame, sweeter than pecan pie.

Although the end of the buffet table offered forks and knives, I never made it there. I sat on a bench by the back window, napkins tucked into my shirt and pants. I used my fingers and Binny used my fingers too, as if we were alone, as if no one could see the way she took them into her mouth. More likely, she didn't care.

Pruhar found us.

"I once had a party with no booze," he greeted us. "But it really is an essential device for artists. Sip it, sniff it, act gently confused."

He looked at Binny and extended his hand. "I'm Simon Pruhar." He was naturally flirtatious and had the qualities of a younger man—deferential, earnest. Despite the salty, damp air, his hair was dry and full. He was still very handsome in his black linen coat and cream, collarless shirt. Montrose told me that Pruhar had enemies, but it was hard to believe. "There was talk that Rand was bringing someone."

There was no such talk; I had mentioned Binny's visit to no one. Binny sat on the bench as she sat on my hammock, as if she belonged.

"I was over to see Rand's paintings. They're quite wonderful," Binny lied.

"Simon, stop chattering and get some more coleslaw out here," Rita Pruhar said, stepping out of the crowd toward us. She spoke to him as if he were her son rather than her husband. She had a great smoker's voice, bitchy and low. Short, heavyset, vital, heavily made-up, her eyes were bloodshot. If I didn't know that they were high school sweethearts, I would have had no clue how she had come to marry Pruhar and his cool innocence. Rita Pruhar was in radio advertising sales and had no tolerance for his artistic babyishness, Montrose had told me. She ran the show. She was blunt, and suspicious of anyone who wasn't. She knew all the gossip in New Haven *and* Clinton.

Montrose was very fond of her. He admired that she had no interest in losing weight; he saw this as an act of solidarity with him. He spoke frankly to her when he thought her husband was about to make a financial miscalculation. Pruhar had recently lost money in a Virginia real estate trust a colleague had tipped him on.

"More? They finished that bowl already?" Pruhar whined.

"That's what people do at parties, dear," she said. "Don't punish your guests just because they're hungry."

She wore her own black jacket over a cream blouse. Around her neck was a black necklace with a single polished jade oval hanging between her large breasts. It was simple and severe and pure deep green. She had matching jade bracelets that clasped with a delicate mechanism.

114

She caught me staring at her chest.

"Simon made it. He's got all these kids working for him. Younger and younger. Where do you get them, Simon?"

"College students. They want the experience." Pruhar still taught sculpture at Yale, his first and only job after leaving New Orleans. Despite all his hustling, he was, in some ways, motionless.

"Running in and out of the workshop in our basement. Good kids, but they have no idea what a clean house is, or how to keep it clean," Rita added. "That's why it's good he got that new studio in West River."

"Rand, have I showed you this jade I've been doing for myself? A very difficult stone." His eyes, a hush-puppy brown, blinked rapidly when he was excited, as if by opening and closing them quickly he'd take more in.

"Doing for me, you mean," Rita corrected. She had bold, black eyes that sparkled in self-satire, and tiny fine lines crisscrossing her forehead. Her nails were painted poinsettia red.

"And a new design of diamond-shaped dinnerware for myself."

"For Nieman you mean," Rita added.

"It's not clear where that's going," he said modestly.

"They're in negotiations, my husband and Nieman Marcus," Rita said to Binny. I could tell that Rita Pruhar adored her husband, but Montrose told me she doubted him too. He had sold one sculpture to Joseph Hirshhorn, but had never sold another; he had touched celebrity, but never broken through to fame. After thirty years living with an artist, Rita Pruhar's responsibility was to reality, not to folly and long odds, but she was obviously very excited about a deal with the luxury retail stores. I remembered reading that Mr. Marcus would have been forced to take out a $100 million life insurance policy if he took his company public; instead he stayed in Dallas and kept it private.

"Meanwhile, keep your workers in the basement, will you?" Rita requested. She was ready to get back to the business of her party. "They ruin the kitchen floor."

"Well, make yourself at home. Dance," Pruhar said. He put his arm around his wife's shoulder and crossed the room into the kitchen.

When Pruhar retreated into the buzz, I said to Binny, "You ought to dance. You said you liked to dance."

She looked at me invitingly.

"Not with me," I said. "I don't dance at parties. Find a partner and spin him around."

"You're serious? You're refusing me." She was genuinely shocked and dismayed.

I hated dancing. My grandmother and grandfather liked to dance. Even when my grandfather had pancreatic cancer and lay in his living room too weak to eat, he would ask my grandmother and the nurse's aide to pull him to his feet. Standing, he would have them move the glass table that sat in the middle of the room, and they would go in a small circle around the carpet to Benny Goodman on an eight-track tape, my grandfather leading but my grandmother supporting him. Then my grandmother would help him lay down again.

Binny wandered off. The attention she received had revived me. Nearly everyone was dressed in black and was middle-aged or older. A few dapper men in their thirties, former students of Pruhar's, now graphic artists or sculptors who supported themselves with construction work or carpentry or teaching, loitered near the doors, smoking. I moved outside to the porch and saw Binny choose an older gentleman to dance with, leading him onto the dance floor in the barn.

I heard Burr and his wife Anne before I spotted them. Anne was saying, "It really doesn't matter what you think."

"Best in the twentieth century?" Burr asked.

"Close," I heard Montrose answer. I could pick out his voice anywhere. Gruff, an edge of challenge, a touch of humor, ready-to-go. Eating barbecue shrimp, I hadn't seen either Montrose or Burr come in.

"Brancusi defines modern art in a way very few have," Montrose continued. Did he talk about anything other than art? "At the level of Picasso. A style that says, Modern Art. Taking embellishment and decoration away and substituting pure form. Imagine the shape of the telephone at the turn of the century and now. The influence that made the telephone come out the way it has, that's Brancusi."

"So you like him," Anne said. She was as serious as Montrose, a sculptor herself, with perfect posture, long bangs, and large teeth.

"I didn't say that. I like Giacometti. Brancusi had a natural facility. But the most interesting thing about him was that he quit sculpting in his forties."

"That sounds familiar," Burr teased.

"So why did he quit sculpting?" Anne asked.

"He ran out of things to say." The way Montrose's voice went up sometimes I wasn't sure if it was a question, a speculation, or a truth. "And he had too much integrity. But it shows an underlying weakness in his concept that he would run out of things to say, don't you think?"

Montrose didn't chit-chat. He delivered messages about art. His unmistakable voice carried a punch. He spoke to try out his ideas on people. He spoke so that he could correct himself the next time he delivered a message on the same subject.

"So why did *you* quit sculpting, Harris?" Anne asked sharply.

"He's never really quit, you know," Cynthia said. "I still find these little pieces in his studio."

"My wife's career is the interesting one," Montrose said, avoiding confrontation on Pruhar's birthday. "She's expanding while everyone in New Haven is laying off. You should hear about this new contract she just signed."

Montrose spotted me.

"Rand, is that you? Is that you, Rand?" he said a bit too loud, looking straight at me. "What are you doing at this party? I thought you didn't do parties."

"I wanted to check out the scene. These are my brothers, my artistic brothers," I said facetiously, moving to join him.

The music grew louder. I saw Burr dancing with Pruhar's wife; when I turned to take a beer from the tin tub, I could see Pruhar inside the house pulling gently at his right ear like a third base coach.

"You know, he collects people," Montrose said lifting his chin toward Pruhar with a hint of amazement, a hint of disapproval.

"So you've said."

"He may not even have met half the people in this room before. But now they all owe him. Some feel they owe him a lot, some feel they owe him almost nothing at all. But for my friend Simon, it's a matter of getting enough different dots into his universe so that someday he can connect them. And when he can connect different dots with each other, that's good for him. You can never have enough dots, you know." He said this as a put-down, although his attacks on Pruhar always included a little envy, I thought.

He picked up his Coke can. Montrose walked with a little stoop, as if he were still bent over his desk slightly, getting the best light to work in.

"Who do you want to meet here?" he asked me. "There are many talented and original people in this room." He was putting Pruhar down again.

"I'm just looking around, enjoying the food."

"A night of New Orleans and they don't even have pralines. God, I love pralines." He slipped momentarily into the southern accent of his childhood.

"How are you?" Pruhar asked Montrose, stopping by on his rounds.

"You know, now that you ask, I'm going to tell you," Montrose answered.

"Go ahead."

"My nose is suffering. What they call the barometric conditions are affecting it. You know about these barometric conditions?"

"Not much," Pruhar answered.

"Me, either. It cools off and then gets hot again, well, there you are. And my back . . ."

"Never ask how he is," I said to Pruhar.

"Who are all these people?" Montrose asked.

"They're my friends."

"They're not your friends."

"They are."

"They're not, no matter what you think," Montrose said. "Hey, when you come over next time, remind me to give you back the vase you gave to Cynthia. She's too polite to say she doesn't like it. You shouldn't go foisting your vases on people who can't refuse you."

Montrose's relentless attacks on Pruhar's ceramics-making seemed a little screwy to me. I didn't really understand why he was still fighting, but I knew he'd keep at Pruhar until there was a blow-out. Maybe he was angry because he'd given Pruhar his best advice—quit—and Pruhar hadn't listened. Why didn't Pruhar's face darken with anger and pain? Perhaps he thought Montrose didn't really believe what he was saying. Perhaps he heard something like affection in Montrose's voice, which always had some tease to it even when it was exasperating. Pruhar almost seemed at ease with the antagonism; I suppose that was the price of a ticket for Montrose's company.

There was a commotion at the far end of the porch. I left Montrose and Pruhar and went over to see what had happened.

"There's a woman skinny-dipping," a small, older woman said, her face pressed to the window. "And of course, all the men are interested."

The full moon was softened by thick clouds. My eyes adjusted. It was cool outside, high fifties and the crickets were loud. From the deck I could see the rich lawn and the short, steep path down to the lighter oval of the pond.

"She really is a mammal, isn't she?" Burr said, coming up beside me. "She asked me if I wanted to come for a swim. I asked her if she'd brought a suit. 'No,' she said, 'it's a party.' She walked down the path and stepped into a half-shadow.

Then we could see her laying her clothes on the ground near the path."

A group of five or six men were staring down at the water fifteen yards away from which Binny, naked, was just emerging. A pair of floodlights threw their wattage into the low fog. When she moved between the two giant copper beech trees, you could see her silhouette. She shone like an otter. She'd said she wanted a good time.

I felt betrayed, standing there on the deck with Burr and Pruhar. I imagined some men feeling proud in this situation, but I was angry. I was sure she knew the crowd she'd attracted. She didn't mind any of us looking at her.

"Don't fear happiness," Burr said to me. "That's what she said to me before she went down to the water."

"I'll bring you a towel," I shouted. I knew then I wasn't going to be in any mood to paint her when we got home.

"You don't need to," she called back. Ten yards from us, she stopped to pick up her clothes where she'd laid them on the ground.

"You want an audience, you have one." Everyone on the deck was now looking at me.

"Great prettiness, strongly made," Burr whispered to me, enjoying the drama.

Gleaming, she came a few more steps up the path top-less, carrying her blouse—she'd put on her underwear, her red skirt—her hair pressed to her neck. I left the deck, moved toward her. I had never seen her naked; she was flawless.

"I guess it's too late to object," I said.

"I guess," she said, stopping after a few yards to button her blouse, adjusting it so she was mostly covered. "Come down here."

The path had a wet sticky quality. I could hear the party behind me. I was not happy. There was a cool wind and the low bushes gave off a deep pungent smell. Hugging me, her face soaked my shirt. I put my arms around her. Near the water there were low crooked trees. I thought how strange this was, the two of us in the night air in the late October chill.

I knew in some way she was testing me again. She made me angry, she scared me, she struck me as too large, too beautiful, too heartless and obstinate.

Montrose came onto the porch and caused his own commotion. "How old are you, anyway?" I could hear him ask Pruhar. I was grateful he'd turned the crowd's attention from Binny.

"Fifty. I'll tell Rita to make the banners larger for you next time."

"It's a great party. Your wife throws a great party," Montrose said.

"You can't believe what she's got planned at eleven o'clock."

"What?"

"She's got a female impersonator coming."

I was trying to listen to Montrose as we approached the house, to hear what he was saying so that I had something to focus on other than Binny. She held my hand, and I was gripped by an undefined fear. I was shivering when we reached the porch.

The fear that made me shake came from not knowing her; I didn't know what she was capable of. Did she have a history of exhibitionism? I was not a prude. I used to take pictures of Pam's face when I was inside her and keep them on my desk at work. I was the only one who knew what she was doing when the picture was taken. I thought of those pictures whenever Schuyler called me a monk. Was Binny's goal to embarrass me, to create resentment, to show disrespect, to ruin Pruhar's party, or take it over? She made me feel like a sucker. She had opened her fantasies to others. What else should I have expected from this woman who had another man? She was not possessable, not controllable.

Then I thought: maybe this shiver is exhilaration. I had always been prepared to resist showing my pleasure. Binny had no such hesitation. She had confidence in her body, the way

121

she carried herself, which was surprisingly rare among women. Maybe I shouldn't have been angry.

Binny was impressive. She was desirable; even half of her was desirable.

When we reached the porch, she offered the crowd her spacious smile. Her violet eyes sparkled. She was an arsonist.

As I entered the house, Montrose said in a low voice, "Now here's the deal." He grabbed me by the elbow and pulled me closer to him. "Your friend Schuyler has pulled a fast one on you. He's tried to shut you out of a group show that might have wanted you."

"Where? How do you know?"

"I know," he said sternly, authoritatively. "I just know. I hear things."

"When? Where?"

"At the Kittyhake Gallery in December." Was this the unnamed curator who'd asked about my painting? I knew the name Kittyhake, but didn't know where it was, uptown or downtown Manhattan, or Brooklyn. "I never trusted him," Montrose said, although he'd never actually met Schuyler. "I'm sorry to have to tell you this."

From his tone, I heard he was truly sorry, but also curious to see how I'd handle this rough news.

"And this Binny?" Montrose said. "She may be more than you can handle."

My heart was pounding away. I was confused. It seemed both my best friend and my date were troublemakers.

⟨✦⟩

Pontes called to warn me that I would be appearing on the second afternoon of the trial. He'd rehearsed me that week for an hour in his office. Still, when he called me to the stand, I felt like a pupil again, as if I were in one of Burr's classrooms getting my work critiqued. With my hand on the Bible, I was now the art on the wall, being judged. I tried not to let Binny's front row appearance distract me.

"Mr. Tabor, what is your occupation?" Pontes asked.

"I am a painter and I work for Harris Montrose."

Under oath, I told Pontes that I first met Montrose the previous August, introduced by Burr. (I neglected to mention Burr's warning before my visit, "You should know he's not a normal person." "He's normal in some ways?" I'd asked hopefully. "Not many," Burr had answered.) I told Pontes that I worked at the Abar Lake studio three days a week, and he asked me to describe my life with Montrose—the studio, the computers, how we shared diskettes, where the work was printed.

Pontes walked me through a series of questions about Montrose's high standards, and how my own views of art had changed over the last year. Montrose sat hunched in his too tight jacket and loosely knotted tie, staring at the floor under his table, a sour look on his face.

"Has Mr. Montrose been supportive of your painting?"

"Very."

"He recommends you to people?"

"Yes, he does."

As he sat down, I looked past my interrogator, taking a deep breath. The room smelled moldy and overheated. The olive curtains were closed. It was impossible to know the time of day. Binny looked lovely in a gray silk blouse. Her invulnerability had always repelled and attracted me.

Barrow stood. Behind the lectern, Barrow tipped his head up and when he focused on me, he looked ferocious. The skin of his temples shone. I was ready to take my lumps. "Have you ever posed for Mr. Montrose?"

"No."

"Have you ever given him a photograph of yourself?"

"Yes, I have."

"Did you give him permission to use it in his *Rape of the Muse* picture?"

"No. I hadn't seen that piece before it was published. He had used my photograph in another of his computer images."

"Your portrait appeared in another picture?"

I told Barrow how Montrose grafted my face onto the body of an infant sitting next to a chimp in a tin washtub. He'd given it to me as a birthday gift, a joke.

"And was it an accurate portrayal of you?"

"I don't usually bathe with monkeys." I saw Binny smile amidst the laughter.

"Did you see a figure resembling you in *The Rape of the Muse*?"

"No, I didn't."

"You didn't? Is that because it's not a very detailed picture?"

"It's not a photographic image. Mr. Montrose is not a photographer. Plus the figures are wearing masks."

Did I believe what I was saying? Honesty is not always the best policy; certainly not in art, which was all about lying, about illusion. Montrose had always refused to deal with the copyright or privacy issues of using pieces of other people's photographs in his own images. He brushed off this potential problem—he would dramatically transform anything he borrowed. My answer was a gesture of respect to Montrose even though I'd been furious, months before, when I'd seen how he'd included Binny. *The Rape of the Muse* was a narrative and I was not relevant to it, even if he had taken my photograph and blended my countenance into the picture. It was a story about Pruhar.

"Your Honor, at this time, so the jury may compare, I would like to offer the picture of Mr. Rand Tabor with a chimpanzee. This will be Exhibit 3." Barrow handed a photographic print to Judge Miller, then returned to his lectern and addressed me. "No one has mentioned to you that the person holding the arm of the man with the knife in *The Rape of the Muse* resembles you?"

"No. The person you are referring to is wearing a mask."

"Do you recognize anyone in the picture?"

"I do. Elizabeth Sanford."

"Has anyone told you that the Muse in the picture resembles Miss Sanford?"

"No."

"Have you ever had a conversation about *The Rape of the Muse* with any artists, or has there been a conversation that you've overheard?"

"Burr and Montrose once . . ."

"That's Mr. Miles Burr, your former art school professor and a friend of Mr. Montrose's, is that correct?"

"That's right. Burr thought the picture was sentimental, despite its subject matter."

"During their conversation, did Mr. Montrose explain the allegorical meaning of the picture?"

"No."

"On prior occasions, did he explain it to Mr. Burr or to you?"

"Harris Montrose doesn't usually explain his pictures to me." I remembered going to Abar Lake in the days following the *Vanity Fair* publication. Although he'd grafted Binny's face onto the body of another beautiful woman, I was so angry about his using her as the Muse, I couldn't even talk to him about it. She might have accepted the honor of appearing in his picture, but he hadn't asked.

"Did Mr. Burr say anything else to Mr. Montrose during this conversation?"

"He suggested that the next time Mr. Montrose was tempted to include a likeness of someone he knows in a picture, he should hit that person in the mouth instead."

"During the time you've known Mr. Montrose, has he ever hit anyone in the mouth?"

"No."

"Did Mr. Montrose ever hit anyone at all?"

"Not that I know of."

"I have no further questions. Thank you."

Looking at Montrose, I remembered the birthday gift he'd given me in January to try to make up with me. He had cast a sliver of gold into a fingernail and passed it to me on a tiny pad of cotton. "You know the Chinese had these very long nails they used to dip into opium," he said. That was typical of Montrose, an odd historical detail had caught his attention and drove his creativity.

I loved Montrose. Nothing less than love could have kept me working in his studio that month as I tried to reach Binny on the phone to explain. I loved him because he challenged everything and everyone, demanded attention, uttered heresies with none of the fashionable cynicism of so many artists. He had a buried charm of which he sometimes offered me a glimpse. I suppose I expected he would eventually turn on me if he disapproved of something I was doing—although I incorrectly guessed it would be about my painting and not about my relationship with Binny—but I also felt he understood me.

Barrow sat down and Pontes returned to the lectern. He led me through the schedule of Pruhar's visits over the past year, their decreasing frequency.

"Have you been involved in discussions with Mr. Montrose and Mr. Pruhar concerning responsibility for works of art?"

"All sorts of discussions take place all the time in Harris Montrose's studio," I said.

"Have you ever been part of a conversation about the sources of inspiration that an artist has?"

"Yes, many times."

"And what was Mr. Montrose's view as to what constituted *his* source of inspiration for his computer pictures?"

I thought I understood some of the strange reasons Montrose had for making his picture. Yet even when his beliefs and opinions were not rational, the conviction with which he held them was. Montrose had turned the suit brought against him into a fight about the distance between high and low art. I shouldn't have been surprised; he did the same with all his disagreements.

"The world of nature, the contemporary world, his sculpture, artworks going back to antiquity, current politics. You name it."

"Did he ever indicate to you that he worked on the computer to depict his personal likes and dislikes of people he knew?"

"No."

"You said that Mr. Pruhar visited Mr. Montrose's studio less often over time. What was the source of irritation between them?"

I could have told the whole world the source of their squabbles. I could have told them the whole truth and nothing but the truth, but it would have sunk Montrose. I would have surprised everyone by explaining that this disagreement had everything to do with ambition and control and little to do with ceramics. Pontes wanted me to get nasty about Pruhar. He wanted me to say Montrose's former friend was rivalrous and had a way of getting what he wanted. That he was an amoral schemer. That Pruhar was an unpredictable mixture of masochist and street hustler. That he had a killer instinct that served as his personal narcotic and made him smile gently. The truth was that around Montrose, Pruhar lost definition and acted long-suffering. At least until he activated his topnotch survival skills to give his career some fancy new action through this suit.

In the hideous atmosphere of the courtroom that day, it must have been impossible for anyone who didn't know the two of them to understand how and why they'd remained friends for thirty years. It was impossible for me to understand how artists remained friends for *six* years, the anniversary I'd reached with Schuyler (whom I'd barely spoken to since the Kittyhake show before Christmas). But as I sat on the hard wooden chair, the hollowed seat curving my legs together, I realized that Montrose never gave Pruhar credit for rescuing him from New Orleans. Montrose never admitted that he had been impressed for thirty years at how Pruhar had tested himself against the world. Montrose would never admit now that Pruhar had been a truly good friend—he had been Montrose's conduit to other artists, dealers, buyers, critics. Montrose had turned against Pruhar before the picture. He had not expected Pruhar to retaliate through a lawsuit.

"I don't know," I answered Pontes. "Private matters. Accusations. Long memories."

"Can you be more specific?" Pontes asked.

"Not really."

All the jury needed to hear was that they shared all their woes and happy moments, but I didn't get a chance to say this.

Pontes had me state for the record that I never believed *The Rape of the Muse* to be "true." He had me reemphasize that I didn't think Pruhar was a rapist or a barbarian or a criminal. The picture hadn't made me reappraise my view of either Pruhar or Montrose, I told the court.

"Do you know anybody who reappraised their views as a result of seeing the picture?" Pontes asked.

"No."

"Did anyone ever tell you that they believed Mr. Pruhar carried a knife?"

"No."

"Thank you, Mr. Tabor."

I stood and left the witness box, passing between Montrose's and Pruhar's tables, swinging open the wooden gate to the gallery section and hurrying down the aisle.

CHAPTER 7

Binny arrived late on the Friday afternoon following Pruhar's party and her swim in his pond. She'd put off a writing assignment and driven to New Haven to make amends.

"You know why I came back?" Binny asked.

"Why?" I played along.

I made her an omelet and we shared a bottle of Chianti, talking awkwardly, as we sat in my studio watching the reddening November sun slide across the window facing downtown.

"Because I've never met a man who had pictures in frames. Most men don't have any art, or maybe some old posters. They have three dishes, all their clothes in one drawer."

"I do the framing."

"And the painting," she said. My cat had been frantic when I came in from Montrose's just a few minutes before Binny arrived. I'd been gone since early in the morning and he scrambled around, mewing and pawing. But when Binny swung on the hammock, Occo curled up on his favorite green rocking chair and fell asleep.

"Do you find me sexy?"

"Of course," I said.

"You said that too quickly."

She swung in wide arcs. With the window open to the cold air, sounds floated in, a young girl singing, a car motor, a slammed door. My view looking south was one of rectangular masses, of stacked and winking lights.

I climbed onto the hammock next to her. In the middle of my canvases and the four white walls, we weighed it nearly to the floor, but with a little bounce. Her violet eyes got filmy and her neck went pliant. She drew her blouse over her head, stopping for an instant caught inside, teasing me, available to be taken advantage of. Binny objected to my getting up to pull down the shades; she required no privacy, she said. The glare from the streetlight made her sharp and vivid. From her evening swim, I knew she enjoyed being naked. I could have come up with reasons why we connected, but the truth was I had no idea other than that she was lustful and I was lustful. She had every erotic intention I had from the moment I approached her in that New York classroom.

Topless, we sat facing each other in the bright light, at least two of our four legs touching the floor at any one time, bouncing, the rest of us intertwined, holding on to this Mobius bed. Scales of paint stuck to her bare feet. Her cold thumb ring felt good at unexpected moments. I could tell it was important that I adored her.

We rolled off onto a blanket. On top of me, her hands stayed on my shaky shoulders, my hands supporting her ribs, and then her beautiful small breasts. I explored with my fingers from her chest to her lower belly. Her underwear was ratty. When I slid down to take it off, she said, "When you called you said you were ready to paint me."

"I changed my mind," I said cruelly. But I was not a good liar; most artists aren't; our imaginations don't move in that way. I wanted to tell Binny I loved her. I wanted to tell her that I loved her more than any man in New York could. "Maybe you could send me a photo and I'd reconsider."

"You don't need a picture of me. You need me," she said.

My impulse was to make her promise, swear in six ways not to see him again, never to return to New York. But I knew this was wrong and hopeless. Binny and I were already in motion under different conditions than I might have liked, and I was in no position to complain.

I slid back up to kiss her and lick her closed eyelids. My insteps moved along her smooth legs as I slid inside her. The way she bent made me worry for her spine. For twenty minutes she was alive all over my body. Binny believed in sharing her physical splendor, in primitive longing and sound-making, in pursuing delight, in laughing at the comedy of pleasure, in her own inside smells, and even, perhaps, in romance.

"Someday you might hate me, but you'll always want to be naked with me," she said. This made me unhappy because I knew both parts were true.

"Are you ready to paint?" she asked.

Did she know this was what I was thinking from the orientation of my penis? I wanted to love her. I didn't know what she was doing with me, and I felt vaguely sorry for myself for having waited to call her. But I also felt lucky.

That I was longing for her even while she was with me should have been a hint of how I felt.

I carried the mattress down from my loft, balancing it on my shoulder as my left hand gripped the banister, and placed it against the wall under the tall window. I arranged some pillows. I went to the sink to get Binny some ice water, and when I returned she lay on her side and was very beautiful. Her naked relaxation came from being given an enormous amount of attention at a young age, I surmised. She asked me to open the window wider, and a line of cool air flowed over us. She propped her head on one hand, her dark hair brushed with light, and pointed out dust balls in the corners, given greater shape and volume by cat hair. She pointed at the empty paint tubes under the radiator. She asked me about what appeared to be garbage in the corners: torn newspaper and magazine pictures, unwashed paintbrushes erect in empty chick pea cans. I hadn't swept the floor in three weeks because cleaning Montrose's studio every other day was enough.

Like a cat, Binny smelled things. Her nose was extremely sensitive. She smelled olives and lemons, the river four blocks away, vanilla, new beagle puppies born in the apartment below mine. She smelled the New Haven Horse Patrol, and when a cigarette smoker passed on the sidewalk below. The Indian woman downstairs must have been cooking and odors drifted up—cardamon, asafetida, black mustard, tumeric—which made Binny ecstatic. I felt as if I had tricked her and she had tricked me, there was some trick being played, because we were carrying on despite the obstacle of her man in New York.

While I painted her, I felt as if we were far from civilization. I worked fast, impatient, wanting to finish (although I knew it would take days, perhaps weeks), wanting to show my new work to Montrose. I asked her to stand, to pose. I had questions to ask her: how did she come to review rock bands? She'd told me she would "go to hell" to see a good show, but did she really believe there was a hell? Did she sing secretly? What about write her own music? Half the painters I knew wanted to be guitarists, did she?

I was born with this internal idea of forms that give me pleasure. But for half a year before Binny, I'd lost the ability to discover these forms in my own work. With her in front of me, I re-experienced the joy I'd always had painting. She was, after all, my muse.

She wanted to know about Schuyler. I told her he had an athlete's grace, a boxer's swollen hands. I told her that people who didn't hate him immediately found him compelling. She wanted to know the longest we'd gone without speaking? Did we argue much? Was he any good as a painter? Was he as good as I was? She presumed he wasn't, and she wanted to know if he was jealous of me; and I decided not to tell her about the Kittyhake Gallery show which I'd learned, since Montrose passed me the news, Schuyler had been accepted into.

My floor was a palette of paint smears—as close as I ever got, Schuyler liked to joke, to abstract art. I'd always thought there needed to be a painting of a woman slipping a blouse over her head. It was the pose of infidelity to me. Binny let her head hang down and her arms hang loosely. I asked her to try on my shirt and raise her arms, and bring her arms up and away

132

from her body, slipping the shirt on slowly, again and again. She smiled and told me she enjoyed being a collaborator.

She told me more about Timmy as I painted. She believed a hundred times over that this lost autistic boy could be improved with love. It was never too late. If he got more at home, all the better, but during her visits she would give him all she had, and maybe he could recover partially, learn some words, learn to get along with other children instead of kicking and biting them. I wondered if she thought of me the same way: with attention, I too could be helped.

It made no difference how she thought of me: I was painting again.

Before dawn, she asked to go for a drive. We drove past Yale-New Haven Hospital to the Long Wharf docks where giant piles of limestone shone in the dark, past the twenty-four-hour donut shops, the Dominican carnicerias, the gay dance clubs in the old brick warehouses, the neglected areas of New Haven that I found my way to when I couldn't work. I drove her past the old rifle factory at Winchester Avenue where thousands had spent long days manufacturing "The Gun That Won the West," and the diner in Newhallville where at midnight I ordered eggs over easy, toast, and hash browns for $1.99. We left town and toured the Quinnipiac River in North Haven, and then turned toward the Long Island Sound. Binny asked me to show her places unlike those she might see in New York. We headed back along the windy coast to Guilford where the white lines of rough surf hit the seawall hard. We walked up and down the wide street of that little town, window-shopping, the only tourists at seven AM. We picked up a mushroom-shaped Portuguese sweet bread at a tiny bakery that was just opening, and picked at it with our fingers. Then we headed back to New Haven, barreling along, Binny driving, her foot steady and strong on the accelerator, eyes dazzling.

She was returning to New York in the late afternoon to review a band she'd seen once before. "The band can't play in time. It's got a little bit of a sense of humor, but there's really a desperate feeling to it. The lead singer is this whiplash clown with a sore throat." To be a critic, Binny told me, you needed to be the right age with the right credentials and the right vocabulary, and you needed a strong desire to memorialize the dismal and ugly. On paper, she was harsh and spared no insult. I'd reread the reviews she sent. Her writing interested me; her words took me by surprise She liked lead singers who were ambitious. "I like to hear them sing about the girls they fucked or wanted to fuck and didn't. That regret, that longing," she said, as she found a parking spot outside my building. She had no time for girl bands, no sisterly affection.

When we got inside we were still hungry. We had some plums and Gouda cheese and we finished the rest of our sweet bread. She made me feel happy and expectant. I enjoyed the way she walked, moved her hands, smoothed her hair. When I painted her this time, I was naked too.

I was ready for Montrose to look Binny over, give me his opinion.

❦

"Come in, you don't have to shake my hand," Montrose said to Binny, waving her in with long pulls of his arm when we arrived at Abar Lake. He didn't even greet me. He instinctively understood that Binny was the point of my visit. He was working with his pencil wand on his computer pad, revising pixels, blurring one image into the next.

"Sit down here next to me," Montrose said to her, staring at his computer. I could hear the Nicorette click against his front teeth.

She wore a black turtleneck sweater and a red scarf, with matching bright red lipstick and low black boots. She sat in the sling-back chair next to his desk. The arms were dotted with bits of dried wax. Since we'd discussed it on the ride over, Binny knew I was eager for his approval and she promised to behave. She'd asked me again why I'd chosen to ally myself with someone whose art was so controversial, a man so often dismissed. She had actually learned quite a bit about Montrose while dancing with Burr in Clinton.

Burr had told Binny that he'd sent me to Montrose. He neglected to tell her how he himself had looked after me from the time of my first course with him until I graduated. Burr's nearly inexhaustible supply of good will did not interfere with his critiques of my work. In his office, he could talk for hours about the weaknesses in a hip I drew, and how it compared to the best hips in history. Despite his sleeplessness and the episodes of dizziness that left him yawning, Burr never appeared pressed for time.

"I'm Binny," she said finally.

"Visiting from New York. I know who you are." He didn't look up.

I drew the swivel stool over from my computer desk, forming a triangle with Binny and Montrose. I tried to look around the studio through Binny's eyes, as if I were seeing it for the first time. Above us the ceiling was hung with lifts and pulleys—heavy, menacing mechanisms. Thick chains dipped like necklaces to the tops of bronze castings which balanced on turntables. Although he liked to tell guests that he was done with sculpture and into computer art, it wasn't quite true. On Montrose's desk there was a tin of shoe polish, a yogurt container filled with brushes, a dish of mink oil, a coffee can of metal files, a white plastic container of shellac thinner, a towel, and a small fan; here was proof that he still worked up patinas, still played with pedestals. Across the room, my desk was littered with Montrose's slides, with computer manuals and disks. Out the back window bamboo grew close to the house, blocking off the neighbors. While bamboo made a wonderful curtain, it grew relentlessly, and I had been out there plenty of days chopping at it.

On the walls near the desk were posters—a Bouguereau from the Williamstown museum, twelfth-century Chinese paintings from a show at the Asia Society, an Eliot Porter photo of a forest—and Montrose's own prints. The room smelled of French fries and turpentine.

One cat rubbed against Binny's legs and jumped into her lap, the other circled her chair.

"Hey, what's going on? Who is she to you?" Montrose asked Scout.

He turned to me. "Does that cat of yours have any personality?"

"Occo? He's a killer."

"How long since he caught a bird?"

"He brought one back for me two days ago."

"To the door?"

"Into the apartment." Occo carried the carcasses up the fire escape and came in through a window in the bathroom, leaving the dead finch beside the bathtub.

"What a luxury it would be for Jake to move in and out of a house with freedom," Montrose said.

"Why don't you let this one out?" Binny asked, pointing at Scout.

"My cats wouldn't know what to do in the big world. They'd get all dirty. And they're happiest here with me," he said sweetly. "If they were out, I wouldn't know where they'd be right now."

"He had a cat who was hit by a car," I informed Binny.

"You knew that?" Montrose was always surprised when I remembered what he'd told me. "Right across that road there." He pointed out the window down the driveway. "Poor baby."

"How do they feel about staying in?" Binny asked.

"They don't dash for the door. That tells you something about how good they have it."

Binny stroked Scout, who had come over for another visit.

"What was all that shaking hands about at Pruhar's party?" Montrose asked her. He still hadn't looked up at Binny, but this was his way of saying he'd noticed her taking in the scene at Clinton. "I've never seen a party with so much hand-shaking."

"I met some people there who seemed pretty nice," Binny said.

"You didn't meet the right people then," Montrose told her. He turned to me. "Pruhar must have some real action with his plates. There were some people there I didn't know, ceramics types, I'm guessing. After the party, he claimed he didn't know who was there. You know Simon is very disciplined. I remember when he decided—he actually decided this—to learn as much as he could every day. And to do it he decided he had to wake up early. So he trained himself to wake up at five AM." Montrose shook his head in admiration.

In profile, Montrose had graying sideburns and oversized ears. As a boy they must have stuck out. "Open that box," he suggested to Binny, pointing with his chin at a small wooden container the size of a cigar box on the desk. I'd never seen it before.

She lifted the lid. Inside, the soft rectangle of red velvet was indented by a white alabaster object about six inches long.

"Go ahead. You can pick it up," he told her. He still hadn't made eye contact. He looked over at me and I shrugged, as if to say she was on her own.

She reached into the box and got her fingers under and around the lingam. It was smooth and translucent, the size of a penis, but it seemed heavy from the way her fingers tightened. I was excited watching her hold it. I was appalled, but interested. How could he do this to her, to me? I was going to stop her, tell her she didn't have to do anything she didn't want to do, tell her that Montrose could be a terrible bully.

What made Binny seductive were the moments when she was thinking of no one but herself. In the gentle, graceful motions of her wrist as she rolled the lingam from palm to palm she was oblivious, withdrawn in concentration. The best models in art school were those whose bodies moved into positions they wanted, not those who tried to imagine what painters wanted. Binny held on with both hands, slid her fingers along it, getting a good feel.

"I like it," Binny said, smiling.

"Japanese," Montrose said, finally looking her in the eye.

"I thought as much."

"It's called a lingam. You know what to do with that?"

"I know what *I'd* do with it," Binny said. "They use it for the obvious?"

"And more," Montrose answered.

"It has a nice heft," she said, lifting it high, showing off. I could see she understood that this was some kind of test.

"I wanted to see how you'd handle it," Montrose said. "For the sake of my friend Rand here."

"How did I do?"

He didn't answer.

"Now don't I get to ask something of you?" she asked.

"When I visit *your* studio."

"I don't have a studio."

"Well, then I'm in the clear," Montrose said. He had tied a felt mouse to a string and dangled it from the end of a long pink plastic pole for the cats, who pounced and chased it along the studio floor. He murmured to them while they played.

"Rand says you began sculpting when you were a little boy."

"You're as bad as he is," he shouted at Binny, gesturing toward me. "What's wrong with the two of you, interested in that stuff? Leave me alone. You shouldn't go around asking people to think back like that."

"Who shouldn't? I ask if I'm interested," she said calmly. She was not easy to disturb.

"Stop it. Rand, make her stop it."

"She's a journalist," I warned him.

"What is it that you want to know?"

Having seen her only seconds before banter so easily with Montrose, having never felt very confident with him, I was surprised how she slid off her boots and tucked her legs under her to listen.

"The story. How you started and how you ended up here."

"New Haven? Here? That was Pruhar's fault."

"We're curious about it. We want to understand the secret. Your calling. Tell us about your calling."

"Okay, listen up because I'm only going to do this once. And I'm only doing this because Rand has his own unfortunate reasons for wanting to know about my past. Here it is. My mother bought me modeling clay. I don't know how old I was. This was in New Orleans. I used to roll it up into balls and throw them around. I finally collected the balls and started to make some figures. I can remember the day when my mother stopped saying "What's that?" because she could see what it was. You can't imagine that feeling. It was really quite a feeling. Maybe you can imagine it. Anyway, I made people in houses and a figure of Gorgeous George the wrestler—he was a great hero of mine—and horses.

"My mother had a friend who was the patron of a local sculptor, and I used to go over to the sculptor's studio and work sometimes. I was just this little boy. He taught me to use Q-tips to mold my clay. When I was about eight, he put a bunch of my little pieces in a shoebox and brought them over to the Tulane art department, and he told me they were good but I might do better with wax. I understood the problem: my clay figures couldn't stand and they were blocky. So he gave me some wax and some metal tools and I worked on my wax for eight months or so, and he asked if he could cast a few in bronze.

"I remember my mother used to try to pay him, but he wouldn't accept money. Every holiday she'd buy him an appliance instead. She'd get him a washer-dryer or a Kenmore refrigerator.

"I used to watch the fight of the week, boxing, every Friday night on the TV in my room, and the TV would get hot and I could melt the wax on it and work it better. In wax, I could move my figures and change them, my boxers could really box. That was terrific for me. I'd meet with this sculptor and show him what I had, relay racers, fighters in a clinch.

139

"There came a time when I didn't give this gentleman my best figures. Once he cast them in bronze they were useless to me—even though it was amazing watching him cast them, how you could take malleable wax to bronze without hurting the pose—so I kept my best ones in wax for myself.

"I was this wild child. I'd work on my little men all day after school, all afternoon and night. My father threw a glass against the wall when he heard how my mother was carting me around to art studios. He thought it was sissy work. My great inspiration was his hatred. His position was clear from the beginning.

"Finally, when I was about eleven, my mother sent me to this top sculptor in New Orleans, Kiko Ramirez. Every Saturday I'd visit him and he'd try to get me to draw and do plaster figures. I told him I wasn't going to do it. He said I'd never be a sculptor unless I drew. All I wanted was a figure to play with—what did that have to do with drawing?"

As I listened I thought: all the early praise and none of it had gone to Montrose's head. His mother, a little crazy according to other stories I'd heard from Pruhar, had been Montrose's confidante, his chauffeur and protector, brave in the face of her husband's agitation. Montrose had been a mama's boy!

"Ramirez did teach me mold-making. Make a mold, put the plaster in water, pour the wax in and it didn't stick to the plaster. I could pop out this army of figures—I liked that. Plaster of Paris: $1.80 a bag. No one learns mold-making anymore. The trick is not making too many separate castings.

"I tried abstract art but I only knew plaster and wax, and they weren't conducive to modern art. I didn't know anyone who welded then.

"I left for art school in California when I was twenty. At art school, these kids would come into the lunchroom and whoever had more paint on their pants felt victorious. None of them knew anything about art, but no teacher ever told them they didn't know anything. You didn't interfere with 'personal vision' back then. It was the 1960's. I went looking to learn about Art and it was clear I wasn't going to learn anything at school. I remember just before I quit, *ARTnews* published on its cover this black and white reproduction of a Milton Resnick abstraction. This guy was a pretty weak painter. But in black and white you realized how weak he really was. And this was supposed to be great art! That was art school: you didn't learn to make things, but you learned what 'great art' was.

"I used to bring my teachers pictures and ask, 'Is this great?' And they would say, 'You're going to have to learn what's great for yourself.' I didn't know good Abstraction or good Impressionism. I assumed it was because of my limited upbringing.

"But I came to believe that nothing could come of art made by people who admired Milton Resnick. And it hasn't."

It would have been enough for me if Binny had been only modestly successful in getting Montrose to talk. I'd never seen him so forthcoming.

If Binny had asked me how I started at my painting, I wouldn't have had much to report. I hadn't spent hours in my room alone, playing with clay, ordering hamburgers and eating alone when the maid dropped off my tray like Montrose had. Despite their dislike for one another, my parents saved for my education. I'd been to college and graduated from a good art school. I had no childhood storms. Mine was a tepid history. My parents were only disappointed I had chosen not to teach for a living.

The little creative genius of New Orleans. What a start— no wonder his work was wonderful! The tiny bronze boxers, muscles originating as little balls, still lived in a cabinet off the dining room. They seemed charming now, but at the time they must have been daring, miraculous coming from a ten-year-old. If only I had started as a boy, I wondered if my work would be better.

"Rand, explain to her the past doesn't matter. It's knowing the moment, *your* moment that matters."

What was it about his voice that let you know he wasn't being completely serious, that he was taking a common view and running with it, seeing if it was defensible, seeing if his listener would respond?

He spoke directly to Binny now. "All through that city of yours there are people who sense the moment, work with it, in it, around it. Philip Johnson, your architect. His nose is up every tree. He knows his moment. How else can you be famous?"

"Where does that leave you?" she asked brazenly.

"I have always been left out. I never wanted to be in the moment. You know why?"

"Why?" she asked, taking the set-up.

"Because the moment doesn't last."

"Philip Johnson has lasted," I said.

"He won't last," Montrose said confidently. "Look at Motherwell. He dies and leaves himself a museum so people will remember him." Montrose chuckled.

"That won't work?" Motherwell's plan made sense to me.

"The museum is funded by selling off his prints. His prints are sinking in price every day. Now there's an irony." He was delighted. The decline of the famous who didn't deserve to be famous was a favorite subject of his.

"That's a problem," I said.

"But if you're not of the moment, you're nowhere," he said, undercutting himself.

"*You* were a hit of the moment twenty-five years ago. And you had a show in New York recently. Didn't you want to be a hit again?" Binny asked.

"I'm not willing to do the work of this moment: your conceptuals, your multiculturals, your videos. You know what? I *couldn't* do it. My only hope is that modernism dies. I listen to these sports talk shows on my radio. The grizzly old announcers talk about how if you quizzed 100 professional baseball players today, ninety of them wouldn't know who Jackie Robinson was. There's no sense of history anymore. It's the same in art. I've lived through this period where the purpose of art—to take old values and reinvent them, find new forms, try for Beauty—has

been dismantled. The 1970's threw it all away. Even Picasso
has been misrepresented. He wasn't for throwing things away.
He was trying to be representational. He believed in Beauty.
"I want Rand here to do work that's less marginal than
mine. So he doesn't feel freakish."

Montrose had told me more than once it was all right to be
ambitious, I shouldn't deny my urges. I didn't have to be like
him—unapologetically reclusive, a dropout—he wanted me to
know. I'd be better off if I didn't have his hang-ups, he said.
He assured me he wouldn't hold my ambition against me.

"What if he wanted his work to be like yours?" Binny
asked, as if I weren't sitting right beside her.

"It would be my worst nightmare, and as a reasonable
person it should be his too."

I had to believe Montrose didn't mean what he was saying;
he was being modest. But I'd also heard him admit, "Most
grown-up artists have no respect for computers."

"Okay, let's go," he said suddenly, rising from his seat. He
always rocked unsteadily for a moment when he stood, as if
he'd been sitting too long. His first steps were shuffles.

He stopped suddenly and asked me, "Do you have a photograph of her?" speaking of Binny as if she weren't there.

"No, but I'd like one," I answered. I knew then that she'd
amused him and he wanted to archive her.

"Well, get one for yourself and get me one," he said.

He walked outside to water his shrubs in the front (he told
us it was important to keep the ground moist until Thanks-
giving) and we followed, pulling our coats on. He turned on
the water at the faucet along the house, picked up the hose,
and moved into the driveway pulling out green tubing from a
tightly wound coil. Montrose was delicate with things in his
hands and he held the nozzle gently. He didn't dash the water
back and forth across three or four bushes as my father always
did. He aimed the spray carefully at his boxwoods and was
patient with each evergreen he soaked, giving it just enough
water until the ground held no more, before moving on to

the next, down the row toward the end of the driveway. He seemed loose, serene, concentrated on his task. His shrubs probably didn't need water this late in the season, but he obviously found this chore relaxing.

"Okay, what's the deal with Schuyler?" Montrose asked.

"There is no deal," I said.

"You've given him permission to do this Kittyhake maneuver to you."

"What's Schuyler done to you?" Binny asked.

"What *you* have to do is say something to your friend," Montrose interrupted. "I'm just telling you my way of dealing with such people. I'm sure there are other ways of handling things."

He was trying not to yell. In the forty-degree sunshine, smoke came from his mouth. He had strong advice, but judged me to be a difficult case. As always with Montrose, there was truth to what he said, but it was hard to discern it beneath the cruelty.

"Your relationship is built on weakness," he summarized.

Montrose sensed that I needed Schuyler, that I'd been seduced by his ambition. Montrose remembered every story about Schuyler I'd ever told him. He had perfect recall of small betrayals, disappearances, unkind statements, peccadilloes. He knew that Schuyler was always late for appointments, that he never paid his debts. He heard me talk of Schuyler's desertion of women. But Schuyler's worst sin, to Montrose, was his relentless pursuit of success.

Montrose sprayed the ferns in the circular center of his driveway where his giant *Green Man* strode. The cold air chilled my hands. I could smell a fire burning somewhere and I searched over the hedges toward the chimneys of neighboring houses. Across the street was a lakeside bench where I ate lunch in warm weather. I could never get Montrose to join me in the sun; he preferred the artificial light of his studio, the glow from his pixels.

"Don't get defensive. He's trying to help you," Binny said, reading my mind, or perhaps seeing my face redden. She and Montrose were new pals. "Why shouldn't you get in that show? Who deserves it more than you?"

She knew nothing about the show, nothing about my competition with Schuyler, nothing about my chances of having a piece accepted, but she was my ally and Montrose had brought the subject up in front of her so that she could motivate me.

"Your friend Schuyler wants to see *his* picture get reviewed, I can tell you that. He's done a bad thing to you here by sneaking around. He's already lied to you," he yelled. "He will respect you if you take care of it. He has the highest regard for people who get things done. Don't make a big deal. Just send in your slides, your piece will get in, and you can act surprised to see him at the opening. Afterward, maybe a few days later, you can talk to him about what he did to you if you really feel you have to," Montrose advised.

"So he doesn't do it again," Binny added.

There were sculptures at the corners of the lawn and a line of smaller figures on the roof, just above the gutter line, jutting like gargoyles. Each piece had its own power over me. It was hard, in this setting, not to take everything Montrose said to heart.

"I remember before you came here you were a phenom. You were respected in New York," Montrose said. He remembered nothing of the sort; he was repeating what Burr had told him. "I told you not to move here and lose your place there. You had a life until you moved here."

He was saying this to protect himself from blame. Binny looked at me in a new way; my modest fame was news to her.

"Schuyler didn't tell me there *wasn't* a show," I said.

"Now you're getting yourself confused." Montrose called to Binny, who was standing in the wet ferns and wood chips at the base of the *Green Man*. "Your friend here needs some help."

"I'm trying to help him just like you are," she said.

I almost screamed at her: you're helping me by leaving me to drive an hour south where you can sleep with another man.

"That's enough. Let's go back inside," Montrose motioned, returning to the faucet and turning it off.

We followed Montrose into the kitchen just as the phone rang. He had a distinctive way of answering. His "Hello," began deep in his throat and ended as a question, as if he wasn't sure someone was at the other end of the line. His voice was louder than a phone voice needed to be.

"Simon," Montrose shouted into the receiver. "I can't talk now. Rand and his friend are here." He paused. "I'm sure whatever you're about to tell me is very interesting but now's not the time. No, not even for the short version. I'll have to call you later."

Montrose hung up and announced, "He starts this guilt trip on me when I don't want the world to stop just because he called."

"Your friend feels left out, that's all," Binny said. "Next time, don't tell him you have visitors. Tell him you're on call waiting."

"That would be the way to go," Montrose agreed. "That's right. He'd respond to that. He respects call waiting."

Since his disappointment at the Cengal show—the few reviews that eventually came out were negative, not even respectful—he had become harsher with Pruhar. He exploded whenever Pruhar tried to discuss his Nieman Marcus plans. He reached into the refrigerator for his ever-present Coke.

"You want one?" he asked Binny. She shook her head no. He didn't offer one to me.

"I'm going back to the studio," Montrose answered. We followed him down the hall.

"I think he really does have a deal happening with Nieman," I said. "That's what he's told the people working for him anyway."

At his table, Montrose lowered himself heavily into his chair, exhausted. "That doesn't sound right. But if it's true,

146

Nieman Marcus may have met its match," he said. He thought for another second. "But then again, Simon may be in over his head.

"Simon can be very happy doing dinner plates. It's the kind of thing he can do. And he may well be able to charm the buyers there. When he really turns it on, he can charm just about anyone, you know. You haven't met Simon, have you?" Montrose asked Binny.

"Yes, I have. At his birthday party."

I could see Montrose's mind spinning. He was thinking hard about where a Nieman Marcus deal could go. If he were thinking clearly he wouldn't have asked Binny if she'd met Pruhar.

"That's right. Very handsome, isn't he? He could probably make the design for cups and saucers, but it's hard to imagine him lasting in the manufacturing business."

"Why's that?" I asked.

Agitated, he started thinking aloud. "Too much work. Too much trouble. Too much time with people he'll think are beneath him. He has to actually get the plates made, you understand. I don't mean one or two pieces. With retailers like Nieman, you take on all the risk. They don't want any risk. Simon will have to mass-produce, which means he'll have to link up with someone who actually runs a factory. That will be hard. Factory owners are real businessmen. Simon's smart, but he'll be in a world of conscienceless brutes."

I wondered if Montrose was thinking of his father, whom I'd also heard him call a brute.

Montrose tried to laugh it off, but I could see he was upset. "You heard he was close to a deal with Nieman? He told you that?"

"That's what I heard."

"Well, you never know. Many people find him very alluring. He must think his art career is over."

On the way back to my apartment, Binny said, "You know I love you."

"You can't love the two of us at the same time," I said as calmly as I could manage. She touched my knuckles splayed on the steering wheel. This had a violent effect and I shook her off.

"I can, and I do."

She didn't sound insane or uncertain. I almost believed her.

⁂

When the prosecution called her to the stand on the second afternoon of the trial, I watched her walk to the front in black stretch pants and a maroon turtleneck sweater, and my pleasure memories were awakened. Seeing Binny from behind was always invigorating. Sometimes I sent her out of the room so I could admire the way she left. I couldn't stay angry with her, and now I felt guilty that Montrose had dragged her into this using a photo I had taken.

I didn't know how Binny would testify. In some ways, she was an unpredictable moralist. She was a person who when she saw a stranger sobbing approached him to ask what was wrong. The morning we'd bought Portuguese bread in Guilford, she wouldn't let me park next to a hydrant. She didn't fear getting a ticket; she worried that the hydrant would be unavailable if there were a fire. Despite her tough music critic talk, her character was based on generosity. She had an insistent charity that included sharing herself. Seeing her again my face grew hot; my skin tingled. To be with Binny was to be involved in a mutual conspiracy. She broke rules and found other rules. She'd gotten to me swiftly and deeply.

"Do you recognize anyone in the picture *Rape of the Muse?*" Barrow asked her.

"Myself, Rand Tabor and Simon Pruhar." When she said my name I felt the sadness I associated with hangovers, a slow-motion achy sort of sadness.

Binny leaned back in the witness chair and surveyed the window, the ceiling, the judge and jury. I remembered the weeks after *Vanity Fair* came out in January when I was anxious to speak with her and she wouldn't answer my calls. When she sat forward, her dice earrings dangling, she changed back into the woman I loved, the girlfriend I'd been preoccupied with in a different way in the fall. The beautiful naked Binny whose softness and intelligence had jump-started my painting. I wanted to rush to the front of the courtroom and kiss her.

"Had you met Mr. Montrose before he put you in his picture?"

I remembered how Binny had acted around Montrose that day in the studio. I remembered her telling Montrose about Park Sanford and his belief that she was the only one of his children who had the reflexes to make it as a race car driver. She was unperturbed by Montrose's manner, and she was hopeful for me when she heard about Kittyhake.

"I had, yes, once, in his studio."

"When was that?"

"Last November."

"So he knew what you looked like."

"Yes."

"Had you ever given him a photograph of yourself?"

"No. But Rand had one, and I presume he gave it to Mr. Montrose."

"Did Mr. Montrose ever ask your permission to use a photo of you?"

"No."

After her visit to Abar Lake, I expected Montrose to be impressed with Binny. A beautiful young woman burning with opinions had settled into a serious art conversation with him. But he was not happy.

"She takes you for granted," was the first thing he said to me when I next came in to work. "And then there's the way you act around her. It's really not something I need to watch again."

I told him she'd gotten me painting again, and he gave a broken laugh. He dismissed my worshipful attitude.

"She's greedy," he said. "You saw the way she worked with that lingam."

I told him about her Dave, the old family friend/lover. He was quiet for a long time.

"I don't care what you want," he finally said. "This isn't right for you."

Montrose's wishes were never negotiable; he experienced them as necessities. Whatever I said, I couldn't sidestep the need to dump Binny in his view. He believed Binny would distract me from my work for him and from my own work. I thought he was being ridiculous, directing his post-Cengal upset at me.

"Did you know that you were going to appear in *The Rape of the Muse* prior to its publication in *Vanity Fair*?" Barrow asked.

"No."

"Now would you tell the jury, please, how you felt upon seeing yourself depicted in that picture. How did that make you feel?"

"At first I felt shocked and hurt. I felt upset, like I was physically attacked."

"Has that experience continued to bother you?"

"Yes."

"Can you tell the jury in what way?"

"My sister was raped, brutally, during which she received a concussion of her brain. I took care of her everyday and she was in continuous pain, and I remembered that pain." This quiet announcement shocked and saddened me. She'd never told me a word of it during our time together. I looked over at Binny's sister Julia (whom I'd met only once) sitting alone in the front row on the left; her face did not register emotion.

"Does anyone you know believe that *you* were raped because of the picture?"

"Objection, your Honor," Pontes interjected. "That calls for Ms. Sanford to know what is in the mind of some unnamed person."

"Has anyone communicated to you on the subject?" Judge Miller clarified.

"People have asked me about it."

"Asked you about it?"

"Asked why I was in that picture. They thought I was being ridiculed."

"Does anyone think less of you because of that picture?"

"By their actions, I believe some people do."

"How have they acted?"

"Some people look at me differently."

"Thank you, Miss Sanford," Barrow finished.

Pontes stood and took three steps toward Binny.

"Has Mr. Pruhar ever attacked you physically?"

"No."

"Do you know anyone who believed that picture spoke the truth when it showed you to be the victim of a crime?"

"No."

"Did you think it was true when you saw it?"

"It included a picture of me."

"What is a muse to you?"

"One of the spirits of the arts, in Greek mythology."

"So the term Muse means something to you. Do you think the picture had a symbolic meaning?"

"That I was being attacked."

"Why didn't you bring an action against Mr. Montrose?"

Barrow stood. "Objection. He can't ask why an action was *not* brought."

"No further questions," Pontes said.

Despite Montrose badmouthing Binny to me in November, I continued to see her. I knew all her faults. She was a fearsome challenge, but I wanted to be with her. Watching her step out of the witness box, I had no such dream. Montrose understood that it wouldn't end between Binny and me unless she ended it, and she wouldn't give me up without his help. When his instruction to me didn't have its intended effect, he put Binny in his picture. Montrose knew she wouldn't respond well to seeing herself in a magazine as the target of a crime—who would? He thought I would secretly welcome the breakup.

When I saw the *Vanity Fair* on his desk in January, I left the studio without speaking to him. He'd never told me what picture he'd sent to the magazine to run alongside the Vidian interview, and this was one I'd never seen. I called him when I got home and screamed at him for including Binny in his picture. He didn't fight back; he rope-a-doped me, he took his punishment. When I returned to work three weeks later (I'd been in bed for five days and hadn't bothered to call in sick), I told him that Binny had finally answered the phone after my hundredth call, and said, "How could you have given him the photo? It's clear who you love." I knew he felt no guilt; he had solved my problem for me.

When she left the courtroom after her testimony, Binny was mobbed. She was, after all, the Muse. Against the polished white marble in the corridor she was vivid in tight pants, lipstick, and of course, high heels. Now everyone appreciated her magical power. I tried to catch her eye, but who was I to her anymore?

I walked out of the courthouse and the half mile to the Yale art gallery on Chapel Street. I wanted to be alone.

∽

In a museum, the world seemed very far away. There were no reporters, no television cameras, no talk of money and betrayal. In the early Renaissance gallery it was no particular time of day and there was no particular weather. The paintings on the walls—even the more dreadful portraits and banal landscapes—had qualities that weren't permitted in a legal proceeding: they had mysterious depth and fading edges.

As I entered the later Renaissance gallery, I was shocked to find Schuyler considering a bleeding Saint Sebastian, arrows between his ribs. My old friend was chewing on a toothpick as if he had just eaten. He looked frayed and hunted. Over the years, whenever I wondered if Schuyler was suicidal, I remembered his advice to a depressed art school classmate. "Suicide is not the way out. You may get into worse trouble." He had an odd religious streak and fears of a painful afterlife which he indulged by keeping a large oak crucifix on the wall of his studio.

Schuyler had other fears I had come to understand. I had once believed that Schuyler was certain about his future; but his presumptions of success were a cover for his insecurities, self-doubt, and a morbid predisposition.

"It's the selfless one," he said when I approached. "The one who lost his face to a picture. The defender of the faith." His sarcasm almost sounded fond. "My God, you've cut your hair," he said. "What happened to you?"

I hadn't seen him since I'd broken his ankle Christmas week at the Kittyhake show.

"You look like a dog who's been skunked."

He smirked. "Has all the publicity helped your career? After all, you are Montrose's apprentice. The insider, the one who knows the true story of Montrose and Pruhar. Has a big fat dealer snapped you up?" he hissed.

"No such luck."

"I'd invite you to meet mine, but you'd have to like no catalogs, no publicity, no support, no sales. No one will give me twenty dollars for my ravishing pictures."

Was he being generous in his way? Was he trying to apologize?

I should have knelt down and gently tested his sore ankle, stroked it. We should have kissed and made up. Would this have repaired the bad feelings? His eyes were red.

"I'm not looking for a dealer," I said.

"That's what you said when you left New York last year. What's up with that?"

"I still don't have much new work," I admitted. He'd known this months before with just a glance from my apartment door.

153

"So use your old work. It's a question of the dealer performing for you. The artist does a little, the art does a little, but the dealer is the one to make you famous. You know that. The art world is like the Olympic fifty-meter freestyle. A fraction of a difference is what matters. You get the gold and you live off it the rest of your life. You get the silver and you're lucky to get a coaching job. The dealer is the difference."

Schuyler's usual power was gone. He used to be able to convince me of anything. The old Schuyler, using his charm and command, got cabbies to shut off the meter and take circuitous routes.

"Anyway, what about *your* nude of the muse? How is that girl of yours, or should I say yours and Montrose's?"

"She was a witness today, you know."

"I knew she wouldn't miss the excitement. She always gave you a hard time."

I remembered describing to Schuyler how good the sex was with Binny and he'd looked doubtful. Schuyler had advised me to enjoy the physical Binny, to take pleasure in her good looks, to be greedy. When I'd informed him that she continued to tell me about Dave (as she did about Timmy), not to make me jealous, but rather to educate me about her needs—she was connected to him by a long history and family ties—he didn't even pretend to care. When I asked him how I could thwart my rival, he smiled. Pushing Binny to change, Schuyler believed, would get me nowhere. Plus, he doubted my motives. He saw my interest in her as limited, and negative: I only wanted to break Binny and Dave apart so I could declare victory.

"We're not together anymore," I said. "Listen, I've got to get home."

"I heard you might have some money I can borrow," Schuyler said.

I was expecting the conversation to turn this way eventually. "Come by my place tomorrow. Let's talk."

CHAPTER 8

Seeing Schuyler at the trial made me think back to the Kittyhake show six months earlier. I'd always been shy at openings. Half a year out of the city had only made it harder for me. I was a snob, but one who was afraid of other snobs. Why couldn't I see my task as clearly as Pruhar saw his at openings? To engage, to be considerate, to be interested in everything and also masterfully polite. Why did I make it so hard for myself? I knew what I had to look forward to at Kittyhake: an evening of everyone vaguely congratulating everyone else. Still, I wanted to have my pictures seen and I didn't want Schuyler lording a New York show over me. I had taken Montrose's advice and my work had been accepted despite its postdeadline submission.

I met Burr at his apartment for the trip downtown. On the B-train, I studied the posters for technical school and child abuse. New Haven had no trains, although there was an abandoned bus tunnel that ran for nearly a mile underground. In New York, an unused tunnel would be home to ten families who ventured out only to lug supplies back to the nether region. Anthropologists studied these types; I'd recently seen a special on public television.

The subway shook with my nervousness; my sweaty hands slipped down the poles, while Burr's albino hands, just below mine, attracted stares. Burr had three or four students with pieces in the show, and he liked being out in the evening.

Evening activity made his sleepless night shorter. He tried to engage me in gossip about Montrose's disappointment at Cengal, but I was in no mood to talk. I was thinking about my first show in New York in a year, and about seeing Schuyler who'd tried to get into this show without me. I was on edge, although I tried to shrug off the feeling.

Burr asked why I hadn't invited my parents to the show. I had to shout over the racket of the train. "At the last show my father said only two things, 'What's that supposed to be?' and 'Never mind.' Both meant that he disapproved." Whenever we spoke, my father wondered who bought art. He never bought anything without doubting he really needed it—even new undershirts or a pint of ice cream. After the purchase, he usually felt he'd been overcharged and was angry with himself for agreeing to the transaction. He was sure whatever my mother bought was unnecessary and a sign of her unconcern about money. His prime example was the bookcase in our living room that my mother filled with bric-a-brac; this was art to her. Her attempt at color was a vase in the den that held two peacock feathers. According to my father, artists were people who didn't want jobs.

When Burr and I ascended to the street, I saw that the neighborhood around the Kittyhake Gallery had improved. A year before you could have shot a cannon from one end of Avenue A to the other and wouldn't have hit a car or person. Now potted greenery sat outside new handbag and furniture stores, and shops that sold sexy high-style silks inspired by Frida Kahlo. Drugs were still a problem after midnight, but the people who had always lived here now came out onto the street: Italian women in housedresses, the Hispanic social club, Yemeni kids tossing pebbles at game boards spray-painted on the sidewalks.

The gallery was in a converted church. Burr and I stopped outside the door. Despite the halogen lights on the dark wooden crossbeams, the gallery had a shadowy, brooding aura.

I'd once told Schuyler that I wished openings had jukeboxes so no one had to talk.

Looking into the gallery, Burr said, "I knew they'd want a freak show." He pointed. "The Sudanese slave."

The first cluster of people inside was gathered around a tall African boy-man whose skin was so black it had a purple sheen.

"You haven't heard of him? He was a slave in Sudan from age seven to seventeen; then a year ago he escaped to the United States and started painting. His English is quite good. Anyway, as you can imagine, he's the new hot young artist in town. That's who you're competing against."

I heard bits of the African's conversation as we walked by.

"It never happened that.

"The bad food they give it to me there.

"We didn't think at all about art. We think about freedom."

I wanted to see his drawings, although I knew what he drew didn't matter. Everyone admired survivors.

My old apartment in Brooklyn had been next door to three Ethiopian men. During the heat wave in the summer of my second year of art school—100 degrees every day for a week, hydrants flooding the gutters, bags of ice sold out of every grocery—they actually closed the windows in their apartment. They liked the heat, wanted more of it as a reminder of home. I nearly passed out the day they invited me in to help fix their refrigerator. The landlord refused to fix it because they hadn't paid their rent; they hadn't paid their rent because the landlord hadn't fixed it.

Burr disappeared to catch up with some former students. I watched him circulate. He did not hold court; there was no impromptu seminar. His best talk was intimate, one on one. If you told Burr something you knew it would not be kept secret, although he never named his sources. Checking in with him, you'd hear the latest about some of the older dealers and collectors, longtime buyers. But he let nothing go before receiving some exchange. His most reliable information came in late at night when he was pacing at home in his pajamas and his charges were out at influential parties name-dropping but feeling insubstantial. Half-drunk, they called in their tips for a bit of Burr's endless encouragement.

I looked for the piece I'd shipped down. I passed faces I remembered. Laughing, gossiping, exhaling unfiltered smoke, old friends came up to embrace me. Frank Drajk, whose girl-friend was a medical student and sent him pieces from her anatomy lab to draw; Denise Duhamel who lived on M&M's and talked with me about the first naked bodies she'd ever seen in her father's dermatology textbook. Conrad Warloe, whose wide comb marks meant he was out to make an impression. They clasped my hands and whispered "Welcome back" as if I'd been locked in an asylum. They asked if I was still in touch with Schuyler, "the man with the golden arm" as Frank called him.

I found my painting, *Disappearance*, in the far corner of the room. Before I started my painting of Binny, I'd been working on what I called "counter-representational" art. The art of absence. They were pictures of where people *had* been. I'd done paintings of talcum footprints, slewed sheets, water after a dive, empty shoes that still held their owner's weight and balance. What was no longer there told you everything about what had been there, about invisibility and materiality. I'd believed there was a force in what had vanished. *Disappearance*, the one the judges had chosen, was almost two years old and reminded me of all I hadn't done since. It was hung in a small alcove and well lighted. My biography, typed on white paper next to it, listed me as one of the *New York Times*' twenty-five to watch in 1998. But it was two weeks before the new millennium began, and I wasn't from sub-Saharan Africa.

The painting made me miss Binny. Unlike my art of absence, my new paintings were about flesh, Binny's in par-ticular. My new style consisted of capturing Binny in motion. Like her, my new work had an opinion: be simple, be direct.

158

She'd called me that morning to let me know she would miss the opening and to apologize. She was in Albany, visiting her sister and Timmy. "We had this popcorn breakthrough last weekend," she said. "Instead of just giving him a snack, I got this picture of the popcorn package laminated for him. And if he points to the wrapper, he gets a few popcorns. So here's the breakthrough. I keep the picture by the cupboard. He reaches up, takes the picture and goes to his chair and says, 'Pop, pop.' He associated the sound and the picture. That's like four steps of progress."

She talked for ten minutes about the latest concert she'd been to, and ran down the newest list of beefy male high-energy tuneage she was reviewing while she was upstate. I thought she was showing off when she went into detail about guitars: Ibanez Tube Screamers for distortion, Boss DD-2's for delay, RV-2's for reverb. Before we said goodbye—it was a sad call and made me want to see her—she asked if I was planning to speak to Schuyler at the opening. She knew I was not looking forward to seeing him, and was in no mood for reunions. I was tired of taking care of him, making excuses for his bad treatment of me. I told her I wasn't.

Having found *Disappearance*, I wandered into the next room. "He's talented but fucking deluded." I hadn't heard Schuyler approach, but I recognized this voice behind me. Schuyler found me staring at a tight photo of an orange golf ball held between two enormous fingers meant to make the ball look sexy, dimpled, curved.

When I turned around I saw that my old friend's black leather jacket hung loosely on his skinny frame. He'd lost weight and his hands shook slightly. Judging from his appearance, his luck had run away.

"I'm trying to quit smoking," he said. He saw me spot the Dunhill pack bulging from his coat pocket. "That's just in case I really need one."

The last time Schuyler tried to quit, he carried a deck of cards that he took out and shuffled over and over with one hand when he felt a craving. His emaciated look meant he was low on cash. I knew that when he was poorest, he sometimes woke in the middle of the night dreaming people were stealing his money. But I also knew Schuyler to rip off others; Schuyler chose apartments with imperfections so he wouldn't have to pay his rent; he asked for water damage to be repaired before he anted up. When I'd spoken to Madeline she reported that the IRS was looking for him, which might have explained why he had gone missing.

When I saw him, my first vengeful thought was to call the IRS and spill information about Schuyler's habits, how he'd once spent his entire paycheck on Beluga for a new girlfriend, about the money he spent on the cigarettes he loved so much he smoked in the shower. Schuyler had his addictions, and decency and trust were not among them. Hadn't Schuyler said to me, "Honesty is good only in art, not in artists. It makes them unbearable." I should have known that he would turn on me, not only on his girlfriends who at first thought he was agreeable to anything.

I had never disapproved of Schuyler's ways when he'd been a reliable friend. He had, after all, been an altar boy before he was a boxer. He looked innocent with those long lashes. I remembered Schuyler's father putting his hand on my shoulder the afternoon we met, and telling me his son was bound to be a failure. "Don't misunderstand me," Mr. Schuyler said in his strangely nasal voice. "Arden's a good speaker and persuader, but he is as slanted as the truth. He can't be a painter. He doesn't have the fight in him." Schuyler Senior had thick eyebrows and a slender nose.

Still, there were plenty of times Schuyler had been good to me. He would have claimed that he'd saved my life. Two years before, I'd gotten involved with a waitress who, after sleeping with me for a month, informed me she'd gotten married just before meeting me. Mary wore a ring but hadn't mentioned it; her eyes asked for trouble so I ignored all the signs. She had wanted to be a singer and I had encouraged her. We took walks around the city late at night after she got off work, and we'd end up undressed at my place for an hour or two before she had to leave, claiming she had to be up early for her second job, or for a voice lesson. The same day I learned about her husband, he found out about me. He worked nights at a greyhound track outside Trenton testing dog urine for drugs. He was an expert at forging breeding histories, Mary told me. He hung around with a bad crew. When he came into the restaurant an hour before closing one night, I waved goodbye to Mary and went into hiding. Schuyler had an underground railroad of old girlfriends who put me up, a night here, three nights there. The super at my building reported that Mary's husband had come by one day, armed, threatening to kill me if I ever saw Mary again, and after that Schuyler took to telling people he'd saved me.

But at Kittyhake I found myself doubting everything Schuyler had ever said to me. His disappearances, which he'd once told me were trips to care for his mother, suddenly seemed ominous. Why was the IRS after him if he had no money? Maybe he was involved in narcotics traffic. Maybe he was laundering money for one of his anonymous patrons. Shouldn't I have seen it coming from this latest set of paintings? He explained those abstract pieces as "newly urban." They were half-empty canvases, colors separated by black lines, black gestures. A flurry of brushmarks without underpainting. They were a metaphor for the recent Schuyler: two layers, a knot of activity, but always a cover.

"How's it going?" he asked, pulling down the sleeves of his leather jacket. "You haven't called in a while." Now that we both had pieces in Kittyhake, I knew he would never admit to what happened: that he had intentionally not told me about sending his slides to the curator of this show. He'd pretend there was nothing wrong between us. And if there was, I was to blame. He was cagey, evasive. He took quick sips from a beer. A woman with lizard green eye shadow walked past us, looking

Schuyler over. She wore clothes only to show she wore nothing underneath. "Where's Binny?"

"She couldn't make it," I said. I knew the way to get at Schuyler was to attack his work. "Show me what you've got here."

I followed him to the opposite corner of the gallery. I passed more vaguely familiar art school faces. I remembered a woman with a nasty little heroin habit who majored in absenteeism.

We stood by his painting. It was very different from ones I'd seen a few months before. Here was an enormous canvas depicting steels balls obviously shined by an orbital scuffer, next to melons with three holes drilled in each. It had a surreal flavor and was called *Ideal of the Bachelor Pad*. Studying it, I remembered once reading, "When a painter works in circles, he's near madness."

Looking at Schuyler's piece and the abstract work nearby, I understood I'd become a purist. I'd gone beyond Montrose. He, at least, approved of De Kooning. The Dutchman's greatness, Montrose believed, derived from his negotiating the schism between abstraction and figures. But now I was working on a nude and De Kooning seemed sloppy. I was aware of Montrose's growing influence on me. He had a consistent way of seeing, an application of his aesthetic principles. He ordered his art preferences in a certain way and I had adopted his hierarchy.

"God, that sucks," I said to my old friend. "You should have called it Magritte goes bowling."

He took a step back. He twisted his neck. "Who the hell do you think you are talking to me like that?"

He was flushed with excitement now, or he'd had too much to drink. He drank heavily but never liked anyone telling him he'd had enough. I remembered how he wouldn't put his Christmas tree out until March, at which point its brown needles had made his studio floor look like a forest. Then he'd chop it up, stuff it into black plastic bags, and leave it on the curb feeling guilty that he'd somehow failed his mother's full Catholic aspiration.

"This canvas is my event. It's where I act." He was drunk. And when he was drunk he usually felt sorry for himself.

"Is Madeline here tonight?" I asked, hoping to find someone else to speak with, to cool things down between us.

"She can't paint," Schuyler said. "And I can't stand people who can't paint."

I knew he wasn't talking about Madeline. "When did you become an asshole?"

When he was sober, Schuyler knew how to play the game. He gave drawings as presents to collectors and rich friends, hoping to lure them into larger purchases later.

"You got it good up in Connecticut," he sputtered. "A daily lesson in art history. A fat paycheck."

His breath was bad. I was tired of Schuyler's sniping. I owed him nothing, not even loyalty at this point. I was sick of his darling innocence. I remembered a beautiful dog once appearing at Schuyler's studio. He wanted to take it in, but it ran away. Later that day, he found it lying in the street where it had been hit by a car and left to die. He brought it to an animal hospital. He called to ask for money to pay the bill and I gave him two hundred bucks. Two days later, the dog died. Schuyler disappeared for a week and when he came back he was unspeakably sad.

He staggered toward me and fell at my chest. "Fuck you," he said. "And fuck Montrose and his shitty, ignored Cengal show." He threw his arms around me, then pushed me away and standing close, chopped some uppercuts at my stomach. Cornered, I knew Schuyler could inflict punishment even if he was drunk. He would be savage. His skinny knuckles were sharp and well-trained. He would attack without mercy and would probably use his boots if necessary.

He kept whispering in my ear, "Not so hard, not so hard," as he started to hit me harder. I grabbed him, and for a moment we were locked in a rigid embrace before we started to stumble. When we both fell, he gave a false roar. I fell on top of him and heard a snap.

The circle of faces above us looked down disapprovingly. Burr appeared and took from his pockets handfuls of candies—miniature Snickers and Peppermint Patties—distributing them to the onlookers as if to say, "This is part of the entertainment, now move on, take your linen pants and three-day-old T-shirts and move on."

Schuyler tried to stand again but couldn't. Putting weight on his right foot collapsed him. I saw Madeline rushing toward us.

"Rand, what happened?"

"We fell. I think he broke his ankle."

"His nerves are shot," Maddy said. "I knew something like this would happen. Actually, I'm glad it's not worse."

She kneeled to stroke his red face. "He hit an artist," Schuyler cursed, pointing at me. I went to call an ambulance. I could hear him screaming obscenities.

When I got off the phone, I struggled to recover my calm. Agitated, I took a walk outside. I couldn't catch my breath and I stopped several times to stretch my arms behind my head, an exercise that made people on the street look at me as if I was crazy. Maybe I was. But it was Schuyler who had once stolen a check from me and forged it for cash. My compassion for him was beaten up. I'd fought back at a perilous moment, but only to protect myself. My legs trembled. My old friend, whom I should have helped, was on the floor of the Kittyhake Gallery.

༄

I returned to Courtroom 11 just as Barrow announced, "The prosecution calls Miles Burr." It was late in the day, and journalists wandered in and out carrying newspapers, note-books, tiny laptops. I recognized the two who had trailed me to the museum shouting questions at my back. Thankfully, they had neither followed me inside, nor waited for me to come out. Burr walked through the swinging wooden gate, was sworn in, and took the witness chair. I remembered his Groucho line to me after dancing with Binny at Pruhar's party: A man is as old as the women he feels. Whenever I saw Burr, I reflexively imagined that he was still angry with me for turning down his faculty job offer. Of course, when I told him I was accepting the offer from Montrose and leaving New York, he actually hugged me.

"How long have you known Mr. Pruhar?" Barrow asked.

"I've known Simon for nearly thirty years."

"Are you friendly with Mr. Pruhar?"

"Yes." I knew that Burr couldn't fathom Pruhar's initiation of this suit. "Can't he take a joke?" he'd asked me. I remembered Burr getting Pruhar to talk about his youth during a visit to our school. Pruhar had been a serious gambler in high school. He took bets on baseballs pools and horse races. He worked in a jewelry store to support his gambling. He was interested in medical school because he was good with his hands, but he didn't have the grades. In college, he painted a mural on a fraternity house wall and was asked to take a semester off.

"You are a good friend of his?" Barrow asked.

"I would say so. Yes." I expected Burr to speak with a sense of theatre but he was sedate. He was probably tired. When he was young, Burr worked in his bathrobe every night and slept during the day, he'd once told me. Now, with a regular teaching job, he couldn't sleep day or night. He used two doctors for new sleeping pills, appealing to one when the other cut him off. He blamed radiator noise for his inability to sleep, but he also blamed the activity on the street, babies crying blocks away, cabs, and flight patterns. Without his pills he suffered and looked awful. In the last ten years he hadn't done much work. Montrose said it was because Burr had nothing more to say. I thought it was because he was exhausted. What energy remained went to his favorite students whom he rode mercilessly and humorously.

"How about Mr. Montrose?"

"I am good friends with both of them." When I first spoke with Burr about the lawsuit, I remembered him saying, "If Montrose had an Indian name, it would be 'He Who Holds Grudges.'"

"You've seen the picture *The Rape of the Muse?*" Barrow asked.

"I have." Imitating Montrose, Burr had grown interested in computers since the Cengal show. He'd bought himself a Dell and found the Internet. He phoned Abar Lake to tell me about a site that sold paintings by artists from Africa, Southeast Asia, Russia. He enjoyed searching the site by price, color and size. He put in key words like "flower" or "landscape." After the *Vanity Fair* article, he told me he'd searched under "rape" and "muse" and found nothing. These subjects were gone from art, abandoned; they belonged to another, older world.

"Do you recognize anyone in the picture?" Barrow asked.

"Yes, I believe so."

"Whom did you recognize?"

"There are likenesses of Mr. Pruhar, his assistant Rand, and Ms. Sanford."

"Thank you. No further questions."

Pontes took his place at the lectern. He leaned forward in an agreeable way.

"Do you have social or professional contact with a large number of artists?" Pontes asked.

"Yes." Burr didn't mention that he'd trained half of New York's artists and ended the careers of the other half.

Pontes asked, "Have there been changes in the treatment of Mr. Pruhar by artists you know of since the publication of this picture?" Pontes had done his homework; Burr knew all the hidden nerves and corruptions of the art world.

"People have come to me personally, since I am known to be a friend of Mr. Montrose and Mr. Pruhar, with questions about the two of them. I have, on occasion, asked them why they don't go talk with Montrose or Pruhar about their questions. Many people have been interested in the picture and the ideas it represents. But most people are afraid to talk to Montrose or Pruhar. They would rather talk to me. Not that I blame them."

"So you haven't personally seen Mr. Pruhar mistreated or spoken of badly by people known to you?"

"No."

"Do you believe that the picture was true insofar as Mr. Pruhar is a rapist, carries a knife and attacks half-naked women?"

"No."

"No further questions," Pontes said, sitting down.

CHAPTER 9

Montrose must have had some intuition that I'd be alone that final Friday night in December. I'd been upset by my run-in with Schuyler and his broken ankle. I was having trouble finishing the last details on some adjustments to a frame when Montrose bellowed the length of the room inviting me to stay for dinner, asking me to help Cynthia with the preparation and the clean-up. Having never been invited for dinner before in my four months on the job, I wondered what would be served. Montrose ate very few foods: steak, roast beef, French fries, chicken livers, rice, cakes with white frosting. The only green on his meal plan was hearts of lettuce with olive oil. When he sent me out for French fries and a chocolate milk shake at lunch, he'd say, referring to Cynthia, "Don't tell her what you brought me." When I smuggled in the sealed brown bags, he'd tell me, "I'm not allowed to eat this."

"Why not?" I'd ask.

"You don't really understand her, do you?"

Cynthia was in the kitchen chopping squash when Montrose and I walked in from the studio at four-thirty PM. She stood near the sink, wearing a red apron over an olive green blouse. Her feet were bare on the dark wood. The kitchen was at the front of the house and from its windows I could see the lake. The public landing, far across the water, was empty except for a father and his two little boys throwing bread to the ducks. With the windows open a crack, I heard excited screams floating over, fake crying, a few laughs, the sharp tone of warning. The kitchen was painted a forest green and always felt warm, a rocking chair in the corner, Burr's print over the butcher block table.

"Rand's staying for dinner," Montrose announced.

"That's wonderful. Are you going to get ready?" Cynthia asked. "Our guests will be here in half an hour."

"Do I need to wash my hair?" Montrose asked.

"Only if it's dirty," she said.

"How would I know if it's dirty?"

"You can figure it out," she said.

"I'm okay," he told her. He hated showers and tried to avoid them. He preferred baths, once letting on that Cynthia used to wash his hair when they were younger. "When she still took care of me," he said.

Every few months, they had dinner with the Pruhars and the Burrs, who drove up from New York. Rotating houses, it had been a ritual for years. Sometimes they invited other guests—when there had been an argument between one of the couples, when one spouse was out of town and an odd number seemed unsteady—but not usually.

"You know it's almost Rita's birthday, so this is a birthday dinner," Cynthia said. "She's turning fifty-one on January 8th."

"I didn't know," Montrose said. "Nobody told me that."

I wasn't good with dates either, which in part explained why I despised other people's birthdays. If I gave a gift spontaneously in November or March, why did I need to come up with bright ideas for a present on one particularly difficult-to-remember date in September? I saw that Cynthia took matters into her own hands when her birthday approached. Pam used to wait for me to fail her and then lecture me about women's feelings.

"All these birthdays so close together. Anne's birthday was last month. Everyone's getting so old." Cynthia sighed. She looked around at her black granite counters covered with packages and plates. For Montrose, she peppered a steak. For her guests, she was trying swordfish with a sauce featuring mangos and grapefruits. She used sharp knives and tasted off the edge of her spoon. Her upper arm vibrated when she chopped. She refused to use cookbooks, but clipped recipes from the *Times'* food page, taping them to index cards she filed in a small metal box. She instructed me on how she wanted the table set.

Montrose, who played the market just like his father once did, had spent the week shorting Sotheby stock. He said there was nothing sweeter than watching a venerable art institution lose money and Sotheby's was the worst of the art world, as far as he was concerned. The month before, he'd seen a woman leaving Dunkin' Donuts wearing a Sotheby's shirt and had yelled, "Is your shirt for sale?" She laughed in a worried way, got into her car and drove away from this crazy man yelling at her at seven-thirty in the morning. He called Sotheby's, bought himself one, and on the morning he called his broker to bet against the art house, he actually wore his shirt for inspiration. "You know Sotheby's owns nothing," he said. "Not the buildings where it holds auctions in New York and London and Toronto, not the chairs the people who are bidding sit on, not the art. What a ridiculous company. I could buy a shirt from them though. You have to believe that kind of business is heading downhill. So I'm gonna short the piece of shit and watch the bottom drop." Whenever he made money, he thought of his father, he told me.

Cynthia never bothered her husband about his investments. He'd been making them for years using his inheritance, reading his *Barron's* in the black chair in the family room, half-glasses on his nose, legs crossed, CNN running stock prices across the bottom of the screen. He might have been an accountant, the way he sat there. People thought of artists as financially unworldly, but Montrose invested to relax. He was an idealist in touch with reality. Brokers called him. They heard about him from other brokers. Everyone wanted his money, especially young brokers who couldn't get anyone to take their calls. He listened to them all, played with them, asked their fees. He liked the attention. He asked new prospects to call daily so he could track their picks for a month or two; others he judged immediately. He bought a sulfur mining company in a fifteen-minute call. His memory was exact. He kept no records. He told Cynthia about most of his big moves, trying to taunt her into questioning his wisdom, but she never bit. She only asked how brokers got their phone number.

He was not embarrassed to have money, although he usually didn't talk about it. Cynthia had never gotten accustomed to the inheritance which arrived when Montrose turned thirty-five. She married him when he lived in a one-room studio; the size of the Abar Lake house, its circular driveway, high hedges, and water view still threw her off.

Cynthia took the chopped squash, mashed it, added butter and cinnamon.

"Can you get that?" Cynthia asked me when the doorbell rang. Montrose had gone upstairs to re-shave the areas Cynthia told him he'd missed, and her hands were wet with mango sauce.

From the kitchen I could see the front porch. My old professor was approaching the door behind his wife. While Anne stood up straight to her nearly six feet, Burr hunched. Although snow was forecast, he wore sandals and socks like a gladiator. He looked his seventy years (same as he looked at forty in the pictures Montrose had showed me), and she seemed somewhat younger although her hair was pure white. She looked powerful. Veins bulged in her calves; her neck was wide. She had deep eye sockets sunk beside the high ridge of her nose. She wore huge green bracelets with sharp edges. I imagined her passing quickly from awkward at fifteen years old to striking at twenty-five when Burr met her, to jagged and witchy at forty, to regal and scary now. Anne Burr wore a one-piece outfit, somewhere between a dress and a robe. Her hair was in high bangs in the front, long behind, twisted into a bun.

171

"Rand. Good to see you, kid," Burr said when I opened the door. "You know Anne, don't you?"

A better known artist than her husband, Anne Burr was known for her bronzes of other large women. She was commissioned to make sculptures for the rotundas of every woman's college in the Northeast. She'd done Eleanor Roosevelt; she'd done Barbara McClintock, the Nobel prizewinner who discovered jumping genes. She had a studio in Brooklyn, and when she was finishing one of these pieces, she went to live in the studio, leaving Burr alone in their lower Fifth Avenue apartment. Burr told me proudly that she would work all day in a room with no windows and no air-conditioning in midsummer, then stay up late reading books about her subject, calling him at all hours to discuss historical details.

When his wife phoned from her studio at four AM (during my years in art school, she was working on a statue of Amelia Earhart), he was awake, ready to turn off the TV and talk. I heard the stories he brought into school the next day about his wife's dedication, her interviews with Earhart scholars, the difficulties of capturing psychology in bronze.

She smiled briefly at me when I greeted her.

"In here," Cynthia called.

"Harris keeping you busy? How's your painting?" Burr asked.

Thankfully, Montrose came down the stairs before I had to answer, cutting us off on the way into the kitchen.

"Hey," he grunted.

"I'm going to tell them," Burr shouted at Anne's back. His eyes were black, mischievous, his hair thin on top, curly in the back.

"Don't tell them," Anne said. Her voice was deep, and she kept her arms moving, the bracelets banging. When she looked back at her miniature husband, she wasn't amused.

"Harris will appreciate it," Burr said.

"Spare them." When she shuddered, the bracelets shook wildly and sounded like teeth chattering.

"You'll see."

"We've been arguing about it the whole way over," she said, as Cynthia stepped out of the kitchen and the five of us stood in the hall. The house smelled warm and fruity and exotic.

"My sixteen-year-old granddaughter Rebecca has this boyfriend," Burr began. "A skinny little thing. Well, Rebecca got fed up with him yesterday, and lifted him up and passed him out the window of the kitchen. Just picked him up and threw him out."

"It's not a flattering story," Anne said.

"It's a fine story," Burr said. Cynthia had Anne's arm in commiseration.

"That's some granddaughter you have," Montrose told Burr. "Our daughter is completely normal, you know. I'm not sure how that happened. It's really quite a miracle."

"When are you two moving to New York?" Burr interrupted.

They all rolled their eyes. It was obvious that he asked this question every time he saw them.

"I'm driving in the car with Jenny the other day," Anne said, "and she starts telling me about this new Volvo series. How it's got great power. The lights in the back go from the bumper to the roof, how it's got the shortest braking distance of any car its size. She's going to save, she's going get one. On and on. I roll my eyes. She says to me, 'Safety features, very important. Why are you rolling your eyes? You don't think they're important to know about?' So I say, 'Not important for my daughter to know about.' We're fighting about that now. Why should she care about cars?"

"She fights with everyone. That's how she is," Burr said to his wife.

"Nothing wrong with that," Montrose said.

"It doesn't sound good," Cynthia said. "As a mother, you can't win."

"Our youngest at thirty, a recent college graduate. No job," Anne said.

"This is the deal," Montrose said. He felt that his duty was straightening people out, telling them what they avoided hearing; he'd done this to me regarding both Schuyler and Binny. He'd known the three Burr girls forever. "Your youngest doesn't want a job. Not a job where there's someone who'll tell her what to do."

"That's not true," Burr said. I'd heard him talk about Julie, the youngest and obviously his favorite.

"I'm maligning her," Montrose said. "I'm sorry, but look: she had a job working for that geologist, for that scientist friend of yours. But the way you told it, as soon as they placed a manager over her, she quit."

"She would have stayed if she liked the guy," Burr said.

"Hey. I think a lot of these X-ers are like that, aren't they, Rand? You're almost an X-er." Generation X, he'd informed me, was rich from Internet company stock options but ungenerous; they gave a tiny proportion of income to charity. I was only half-listening as I walked through the kitchen to start up the grill on the chilly patio. I nodded as Montrose continued. "In your daughter's favor is that she works hard. She's just not interested in doing the bidding of others. It's beneath her. Unless it's some awesome person whose bidding she admires. *I* understand that."

"It's just a job," Burr said.

"I say let her play poker," Montrose said.

"Burr told you about that?" Anne asked.

"That she's been reading these poker books and driving to Connecticut and winning $250 a day playing poker against retirees at that casino down there? Of course he told me. He's a proud father."

"But she's worried it won't advance her," Anne said.

"It won't. But she's nothing if not strategic. I wouldn't worry about her. She'll get into graduate school in another few years and do fine," Montrose assured us.

"Her boyfriend's like that too," Burr said.

174

"They don't want anyone telling them what to do," Montrose said. "It's generational, but it's the end of us."

"What do you mean?" Anne asked.

"I mean how can we go on as a country if no one wants bosses?"

"Oh, you're one to talk," Cynthia said. "Never had a boss in your life."

"People will just sit with their computers and do their work," I shouted in through the screen door.

"Those people at their computers will be okay," Montrose called back to me. "The others will just float."

"Smells good," Anne said, and she and Cynthia went to the stove.

Burr poured himself his usual scotch, and came out to join me on the patio. Gas grills made him nervous, flames near tanks of gasoline. I had a little hibachi that I used in my apartment, opening the skylight window to let the smoke out.

Pruhar and his wife came up the long driveway toward the grill. Rita led, small, substantial, round, and tough-looking, all her expression was in her forehead. Pruhar, a step behind, was wiry, not so much from being in good condition as not having time to eat. There was little to be gained from eating, unless it could be combined with a meeting. He was the only fashionable one among the seven of us in his purple silk shirt. He wore a large amoeboid silver ring with a black stone on the last finger of his right hand, a thin silver bracelet on his right wrist.

"We just came from this opening in Boston," Pruhar said. "You know I'm always amazed at how many art dealers are out there." Although he hadn't come by the studio in a few weeks, there seemed to be no uneasiness between him and Montrose. Their friendship was too deep for that. That evening I still thought they were a pair of obstinate men; their squabbles—even personal put-downs—amounted to very little after three decades.

"And Simon wants to talk to them all," Rita said.

"This opening was jammed."

"No one even visits the show after the opening, and no one at the opening gives a shit about the art," Rita said. In this group, she knew the least about painting and sculpture and was proud of her ignorance. Rita said what she thought, and busted balls in the radio business.

"What was the show?" Burr asked.

"It was this retrospective for Tait," Pruhar said.

"That old abstract expressionist," Montrose said. "Who cares about him?"

"Would you let these people sit down before you start with a speech," Cynthia said, poking her head out the screen door. The grill offered the only light on the patio. "Why don't you offer them a drink?"

"I'm supposed to offer you a drink," Montrose said to Pruhar, bumping shoulders with him, football-style. Pruhar staggered backward. "People always hated abstract expressionism no matter what your critics said. Your common man thought anyone could do that kind of art," Montrose said, directing his comments toward Rita.

Burr and his wife sat together on the black leather couch just inside the door to the patio, and the Pruhars went inside and sat on a smaller black leather couch. Between them a low table held the plates of hors d'oeuvres that Cynthia brought in from the kitchen.

"Do *you* think anyone could do it, Harris?" Rita asked. She was happy to be taught, happier still to be made to laugh. Those who weren't really listening to Montrose might have found his seriousness funny, his fearless hectoring rude, his far-out opinions cute. She had known Montrose since his twenties—nothing about him surprised her.

I was expecting Montrose to trash the whole Abstract Expressionist enterprise, to take apart what many thought was the most important American art of the century.

"No, I certainly do not," he said. "It's hard to create an image of wild nature. Not many people could do it."

"You don't think anyone could do a Jackson Pollock?" Burr asked, surprised. I was surprised as well, although I would have thought Burr had heard this from Montrose twenty times. Sometimes Montrose was contrary purely for combustion; politically, he was a Republican around Democrats, a liberal around conservatives. But Montrose might have formulated, or reformulated his ideas about Pollock only recently.

"I think very few people could have ever done a De Kooning, or a Gorky, or some of the Pollocks."

"But people thought they could," Rita said.

"That's why they hated it. It looked easy. But you can't attack Abstract Expressionism because it's easy. You can't say that. It's too low a blow. I attack abstraction because it's irrelevant. It's not about what matters—beauty. If working a painting on the floor makes up what's great in art, maybe Pollock was the greatest. But you know where I stand on that," Montrose said. "Pollock's imagery, not his method, was his real weakness."

He lectured his friends like he lectured me, and none of them seemed to mind except Anne, who left to help in the kitchen mumbling under her breath.

"Harris, where are your socks?" Rita asked, staring at his bony ankles in black sneakers and trying to bring the conversation back into the real world.

"Socks are for wimps," he said.

"Socks are for people who leave the house," Cynthia called. She was listening from her position at the stove.

"The love of Pollock is like Van Gogh's ear, isn't it?" Montrose said, undeterred. Rita couldn't stop him; no one could stop him. "Really it's *our* fault that he cut off his ear. If we'd been able to understand him—we the art viewers—if we'd been savvier and more generous, we would have given poor Van Gogh the benefit of the doubt and he would have kept both his ears. And so it continues to this day. If we don't like new work and think it's ugly, it's our fault, never the artist's."

"Dinner?" Cynthia suggested.

The swordfish had grill stripes, its gray skin wrinkled. I squeezed a lemon before I put it on a plate. I served all the guests red wine as they headed to the dining room. Even the dining room was crowded with art. A long eighteenth-century Chinese scroll painting with calligraphy along the right border hung over the fireplace. Montrose's statue of Medusa stood by the front window. Montrose drank his Coke from a glass because it was a party.

"My wife married me so she wouldn't have to go out or entertain, or go to parties, because she knew I would never go to parties," Montrose said. "People would leave her alone, that's all she wanted. She could study her economics and start her business if no one bothered her. But here she is doing parties. Would somebody tell her she doesn't have to do them?"

"It's good for her to entertain. Plus, she's the youngest one here," Rita said. "She has the energy."

"How old are you?" Burr asked.

"I'd rather not say. Forty-seven," Cynthia admitted.

"My wife says that getting old means getting cozy with your problems," Burr said. "She says a person shouldn't even get upset by their problems after a certain age."

The dining room had two heavy wooden sideboards, one with a silver-framed computer image over it, *Gothic Woods*. I put the fish down next to the bowl of squash. They took their places around a long, dark Indonesian farm table, husbands diagonal to wives, Cynthia and Montrose at the ends.

"My husband loves parties and he always has," Rita said.

"Your husband is a man who can't say no," Montrose told her.

Pruhar sat there, not quite smiling, virtually silent since his arrival.

"He says no to me," Rita said.

"You're just his wife," Montrose teased her.

"This wine is awful," Burr announced.

"It's our wine. We brought it," Anne said.

"It has bubbles," Burr said.

"That's a bad sign," Montrose said. "Even I know that."

"It's awful," Burr said. "How could you let me get it? I didn't know what I was doing."

"Let you? You were in the store. I was in the car."

"Harris blames me like that," Cynthia said.

"Male menopause," Rita said. "I've been reading about it."

"Male menopause is an old wives' tale," Burr said.

"I think he called you an old wife," Cynthia said to Anne.

I went in and out of the dining room, refilling water glasses, clearing salad plates. The swordfish was passed, but Montrose was eating steak.

"Could I have some more meat?" Montrose asked.

"You already have meat on your plate," Cynthia said.

"How did he get meat?" Burr asked plaintively.

"There's a lot of gristle," Montrose mumbled.

"Did anyone see *The Radiance* yet?" Rita asked.

"We haven't been to a movie in six months," Anne said.

"We saw it," Cynthia said. "I thought it was a bore."

"It should have been better than it was," Montrose said. "They were giving you little pieces of insight into that world, but they couldn't quite get it."

"Why don't we ever go to the movies?" Burr asked his wife.

"You don't want to," Anne told him.

"I don't doubt that for a minute," Montrose said. "Sit up at the table, Simon, so we can talk to you."

Pruhar was reclining and slipping down. He hadn't eaten much. He seemed slack; his tone was gone.

"What's wrong, Simon?" Cynthia asked. "You're so quiet tonight."

"He's thinking about that running back who had trouble with his Heisman trophy at the airport. Did you hear about that?" Burr answered for him.

"He's not thinking about that," Rita said.

"They're checking this former collegiate star for heavy armaments and his trophy comes up in the x-ray machine, and someone pulls it out of his bag and breaks a finger off the figure. Simon's thinking how to offer his services to the Heisman winner. Fix the trophy. Make the evening news. Is that it, Simon?"

Pruhar didn't answer.

"I have to think the trophy was made of white metal," Burr said. "Why else would it crack?"

"What *I* was thinking about was how nice these dinners are, how unusual. You know, most friendships go through this constant cycle of expand and collapse," Anne said.

"You're very sweet," Cynthia said.

"Anyone here believe in ghosts?" Rita asked.

"I don't," Anne said.

"Why is it that people who don't believe in ghosts are always hearing them, and those of us who do believe never hear them?" Burr asked.

"Did you know that people call rock musicians 'artists'? I heard it on my radio today," Montrose said.

"Aren't they?" Rita asked. She was the only one leaning forward, arms on the table.

"I mean that's like calling a person who frames a house an artist."

"Creative people are artists, whether you like it or not, Harris," Cynthia said.

"Not if they're rock musicians," Montrose said. I wondered how Binny would respond; we hadn't seen each other in weeks; she was travelling on the west coast. I went to bed early just to dream of her. I had been warned against her erotic insta-bility, but I was desperate to see her, to get her back to New Haven—but not near parties or ponds—to paint her and spend a few days in bed with her.

"So what did you think of the opening this afternoon?" Burr asked Pruhar.

"There was nothing at stake in that show," Montrose interrupted.

"Harris, are you really that competitive?" Rita asked.

"Yes. Of course he is," Cynthia said.

"No, I'm not," Montrose said.

"Oh yeah, right," Cynthia sniggered. "When someone you know gets recognition, you might not *want* it for yourself, but you're *not* generous. You're not happy for them."

"Why should I be?" Montrose asked.

"*That's* competitive," Cynthia said. Montrose had made the point for her.

"Great dinner," Montrose said. "Coffee? Who wants coffee? And we have a great dessert. I got it myself." It was my cue. In the kitchen, I turned on the burner under the coffee. I was so used to doing work around the house, between courses I naturally fell into the role of hired help.

"Imagine that," Burr said.

"Let me guess, a white cake," Pruhar said, finally.

"They usually have four roses on their white cakes, but I got twelve for free from my bakery man," Montrose said proudly. "We know each other. I told him there would be terrible disappointment and upset if there were only four roses. I know him pretty well."

"Other than white cake with white frosting, what kind of cake does your friend recommend?" Pruhar asked.

"I don't know," Montrose said.

"I thought you said you know him."

"I don't know him like *that*."

"He knows him only for his own purposes," Cynthia said.

I brought in the cake, a plate of brownies, and a bowl of fruit salad.

"I hope you don't want that brownie," Montrose said to Cynthia.

"You want cake *and* a brownie?" Anne asked.

"I do want it," Cynthia told her husband. "But I'm watching my weight."

"You look great," Burr said.

"I'll split it with you," Harris said to Cynthia.

She picked up a knife and cut it one-third, two-thirds, giving him the bigger piece.

"God bless you. What self-restraint. What a great wife."

They passed the fruit bowl around the table, as I brought in coffee.

"You really are quiet tonight," Burr said to Pruhar.

"He's always quiet after someone else's show. He wants to know why it's not *his* show," Montrose said.

"What are you working on?" Burr asked Pruhar, trying to engage him.

"Simon doesn't work anymore," Montrose said. "He makes pottery."

When I heard that tone in Montrose's voice, I moved to the door of the dining room to see what would happen next. He had been stewing about Pruhar's ceramics-making since the day I arrived at Abar Lake. What was so wrong with Pruhar's ceramics, I'd asked him again and again, pieces that even Montrose would have admitted were well-made? Did Montrose really believe he could control his old friend?

"That wasn't very nice," Cynthia said. "Don't ruin a perfectly nice evening."

"I'm trying to get him to see what's happening here." His anger was starting to build. The rage that couldn't be stopped once it had begun, which owed no explanations, which rejected all peacemakers.

"By attacking him?" Cynthia asked.

"Have you told Harris about your latest Nieman Marcus idea yet?" Rita asked her husband. "I think he'll get a kick out of it."

Pruhar was hesitant. He began slowly only after Burr begged. "I pitched this idea a few days ago," Pruhar began. "It's for an advertisement, a magazine ad. We would take one of the cup and saucer combinations I've been making, and put it in the hands of the figures in one of your old sculptures. Maybe give it to Adam and Eve. We use some catchy title like, 'The First Sip.' It would show off your work *and* my work. I told the Nieman people that you and I were old friends—the marketing director there is a big fan of yours—and that you'd like the playfulness."

"He's kidding, right?" Montrose asked Rita.

"It would be terrific exposure for you," Rita said.

"There are more deals in merchandise, more intrigue, is that right?" Montrose screamed, sitting forward.

"Harris, what are you doing?" Cynthia moaned. "Simon's made a very generous offer."

Turning to Burr, Montrose spoke about Pruhar as if he weren't there. Everyone at the table shifted uncomfortably. "Of course, he figures his art career is all downhill from here, and in a way he's right. Why not sell ashtrays through catalogs? What more can he expect to happen at his age?"

I saw Cynthia squirm.

"And if you can't be of the artistic moment, why bother, isn't that right, Simon?" Montrose continued.

The room was silent and I could hear the cats searching the dishes in the sink for scraps.

"Fuck you, Harris," Rita said.

"Yeah, fuck you, Harris," Cynthia repeated.

Pruhar simply looked down, then went over and kissed Cynthia on the cheek, headed for the door and walked out, Rita behind him.

The simple, direct questions that all apprentices want to ask are the most difficult to manage. I'd always wanted to impress Montrose, to make him believe that I knew exactly what he was thinking. This self-consciousness blocked my path to serious questions of the heart. To this day, I want to ask Montrose why he attacked Pruhar in front of his wife and their friends after a cozy supper of swordfish and white cake. Was it because what might have sounded to some like a generous offer—springing from Pruhar's enthusiasm for his new venture—Montrose heard as proof that Pruhar hadn't been listening to a word he'd said over the past months: he didn't want to be tied to Pruhar commercially, not with Nieman or anyone else. Had Pruhar, by bringing up their friendship and dropping his old friend's name for profit and glory, shown an unacceptable lack of control? Montrose acted as if this was the final insult: not only was Pruhar wasting his time with tea settings, but now the Nieman Marcus enthusiast wanted to drag him down too. Did Montrose just *need* to attack someone every few hours; was it a form of self-stimulation? Did he really care that Pruhar was designing plates?

Over the years, I've come to understand that he attacked mostly out of a sense of disappointment, when his friends (or I) weren't seeing the world clearly, when he wanted us to do better, but saw no other way to make this clear than have us feel badly about ourselves. He had gone too far this time with Pruhar; he had an unerring sense of people that made him vicious, a natural ability to detect weakness that made him cruel. Of course, Pruhar couldn't know what was coming in *Vanity Fair* when it appeared on the newsstands a few days later. Who could?

CHAPTER 10

On the morning Montrose was to testify, the crows were in tune outside the courthouse. They dominated the treetops like ebony gargoyles, and when they came to the ground they cawed loudly as they hopped over the black umbilicals of television truck cables. They beaked up donut droppings and returned to their overhead perches.

"Trials aren't about principles, you know," Cynthia told her husband on my last day of work at Abar Lake a week earlier. "Even if you wish they were. They're about how you present yourself."

"I don't make a good impression?" he asked, innocently.

"Often you don't. You make quite a bad one at times."

"But you believe in my picture, in the principle of free speech."

"I certainly do. But you still need to try to be presentable. The jury is not a sophisticated art audience. You don't want them to think you're making fun of them."

As I entered Courtroom 11, Cynthia caught up to me and whispered, "I need two cards to hold up during his testimony. One that says, 'You can't do that,' the other that says, 'You can't say that.'"

"And if you had them, he'd pay no attention," I said.

"No, he wouldn't, would he," she said, smiling weakly.

When Cynthia let go of my left arm, Montrose took my right. "She's taking this much harder than I am."

Barrow had the first shot at Montrose, who curled forward in the witness chair. Cynthia had obviously dressed and shaved him; he wore a black silk shirt and had none of his usual whisker patches. His studio was the atmosphere in which he was rooted, the background against which he stood outlined in my mind. There, he was smart, funny, exciting; life seemed fuller when he was making sense of art history for me. In his studio he knew who he was; in court, he was restless and miserable.

"You've known Mr. Pruhar since the beginning of his career?" Barrow asked.

"Nobody worked as hard to start a career as Simon." Montrose's voice rang out.

"How long exactly have you known him?"

"I don't count very well. I knew him when New York gallery owners wouldn't come to New Haven. In our day, you had to bring art to them. Simon used all his might to get people to look."

My heart beat fast as he spoke. Even when he was outrageous, he was spellbinding. I found myself drawn in.

"That sounds like what artists do," Barrow said.

"He was trying to figure out the New York scene from here in New England. I was quite curious myself to see how it worked."

"Mr. Pruhar figured it out, didn't he? He's had quite a terrific career."

"Simon intended to be rich and famous. He believed obscurity was failure. He had a little talent and he trained himself to be just proficient enough to impress a certain part of the art world. He made friends with art professionals."

"So Mr. Pruhar made a name for himself."

"He thought that if only you had the right dealer, you'd be okay. But once he got there, in his uptown Madison Avenue gallery, he saw it wasn't all it was cracked up to be. He should have known, but he didn't want to know."

186

Barrow had succeeded in demonstrating how prideful Montrose was with just these few questions. He was baiting Montrose, trying to make him seem unlikeable to the jury, trying to get him to go after Pruhar even before he broached the subject of the *Vanity Fair* picture. Montrose saw he was being set up by Barrow, but he didn't suppress his impulses. He was just explaining the way the world worked.

"But you made a pretty good career based on the information you gained from watching Pruhar, or that Pruhar brought back to you."

Montrose had always enjoyed Pruhar's gossip; he liked anyone willing to speculate. He didn't like people who only wanted to be liked. He prized instinct and nerve, and so he enjoyed meeting businessmen and restauranteurs and real estate developers, his daughter Lily's friends.

"A handful of artists—your Henry Moores, your Giacomettis—sell to a handful and a half of art buyers." Montrose thought he should explain the artist's life to the room. "The rest of us take turns waiting out on the street. I had a turn. Pruhar didn't really, although he's always had shows, if that's what you call a 'terrific career.' He's refused to acknowledge it's a numbers game. The chances of getting in that handful are worse than your chances of getting into medical school. And it's worse now than when we started."

I had never heard stated quite so openly what I had felt for a year, what I was feeling when I decided to move to New Haven. That the chance for a decent career was nearly hopeless. One needed early luck or head-banging patience.

"Can you tell us the meaning of your cybermontage, *The Rape of the Muse*?"

"I can't describe or interpret it for you since I don't know its meaning completely. It's to be interpreted by each viewer in accordance with his own values, beliefs, and lifestyle. To me, the painting is allegorical. The Muse represents art, which is innocent. The picture demonstrates that one cannot hurt the Muse. Those who attack the Muse only hurt themselves and turn against themselves. This is represented by the dagger pointed not only at the Muse but at the rapist."

"Does the central male figure represent any particular person?"

"He represents those who attack the Muse."

"But no particular person?"

"No."

"And the other male figure, the one holding onto the arm of the man bearing the knife?"

This was the figure that Burr testified looked like me; I had denied any resemblance.

"He is reluctant to join in the attack against the Muse."

"I see." Barrow sounded doubtful. "The physical environment in the picture is in fact a few feet from Mr. Pruhar's studio, isn't that correct?"

"No. That's not true."

"That's not true? Is it any particular place?"

"Not that I know of."

"Does the fountain stand for anything?"

"The red stuff coming from the fountain seems like blood to me."

"What is that supposed to mean?"

"That's supposed to mean that blood instead of water comes from the fountain. When you attack the Muse, you have a lot of trouble." Montrose grinned suddenly. He was a little sheepish, charming. A few people laughed.

"The masks on the figure, do they have any allegorical significance?"

Montrose looked directly at Barrow, suddenly serious again. "In Greek tragedy as I understand it—and I'm no expert, I've never been to a play—the masks were made to represent character, not personality. They had a whole tradition of that sort of thing, and I use it in the same way."

"What is the character that is depicted by the mask on the central figure, the one wearing a trench coat?"

"The masks are to represent evil. But at the same time, inside the mask there is a little human glimmer so that you can tell that the mask is not the face."

"Did it occur to you that some people might not understand that your picture was allegorical?"

"Who wouldn't understand that?" Montrose sat straight up in his chair. He was incredulous. Barrow's suggestion seemed impossible. For Montrose, art was about generating associations. There wasn't much to say about pictures that had no content. He had always objected to conceptual art because it was about the nonexistent, the unspoken, subjects raised but not discussed. In art he wanted interesting, complicated, various; Montrose preferred high diving to holding one's breath underwater.

"Is the original picture, the original print for sale?"

Even in school I understood that art was first and foremost commerce. In 2000, being good at business was the most fascinating art of all. For dealers, collectors, and even curators, money was the first priority.

"It is definitely for sale."

"Why did you select that picture to publish in *Vanity Fair*?"

"Because it was one of my best pictures." There was again a little murmur of laughter from the artists in the room. Judge Miller smiled. Montrose looked at him for the first time.

"When you completed your picture, the central male figure, the one with the trench coat on, did it occur to you at that time that it resembled Mr. Pruhar?"

"When it was published, people said to me that it looked like him, but it didn't occur to me personally."

"So when people said that to you, did it seem to you that it indeed resembled Mr. Pruhar?"

"If I stretched myself, maybe I could see a resemblance. But I've never stretched myself that way." Montrose was an expert at refusal. He couldn't be pushed into sweeping the front steps, erecting neighborly fences, or seeing things the way others saw them.

"Does Mr. Pruhar have a trench coat like the one worn by the central male figure in the picture?"

"I don't know." Montrose shrugged magnificently.

"Have you ever scanned a picture of Mr. Pruhar into your computer?"

"I haven't, but maybe Rand did. Did you ask him?"

"Did you ever use your computer to manipulate a photographic image of Mr. Pruhar?"

"I may have. I really don't remember. I manipulate plenty of people." The court laughed.

"Did you ever see him wear a trench coat like the one in your *Vanity Fair* picture?"

"He's more interested in fashion than I am."

"As to the figure on the extreme left, did it occur to you at the time you were working on the picture that it bore a resemblance to your assistant Mr. Tabor?"

"All the figures in the picture are wearing masks, so I don't really know who they are." Did he believe this or had he been trained by Pontes to avoid being cornered? I wasn't sure.

"When you published the picture, did it occur to you that it might be offensive to Mr. Pruhar?"

"Why would it? He's not in it."

Barrow paused, cleared his throat. "Prior to the *Vanity Fair* publication, did you have any conversation with Mr. Pruhar about the picture?"

"Not as far as I remember. The first I heard from him about this thing was the day he sued me."

To his friends, Montrose was a credible analyst. He was not a lunatic, although he was perpetually excited; excited not in a destructive way, but in the spirit of figuring things out. He was dark about nothing; art filled him with enthusiasm and possibilities. Nor was he personally dysfunctional. He married young and stay married; he had a daughter who loved him; he could derive great pleasure from small events: his cat's unexpected dash outdoors, his wife's latest quarterly statement. His

190

biographers would be forced to explain his particular blindness about this one picture.

"Again, Mr. Montrose, you're claiming that no one in this courtroom is depicted in *Rape of the Muse?*"

"You know, even as a sculptor my figures were never really any good. I never really knew antique principles. I could never roll a rib like Michelangelo. I could never really make faces that were any good. I always had my troubles. I tried to substitute narrative to make up for my figures. I tried to make my sculptures like the old paintings which are beautiful, miraculous, without irony."

I could tell he was on a roll now. He was preparing for an art talk.

Barrow wanted yes or no answers, but he couldn't stop Montrose. This was art Montrose was talking about, and art deserved more than a monosyllable.

"You know, when perspective hit painting in the Renaissance it was so much more magical than the actual three dimensions. All sculpture could do were those three dimensions and so it took second place to painting. And it stayed that way for 400 years. I knew sculpture was in second place when I started as a sculptor, but I didn't know why. When I finally figured out that there were computers around, it was clear that painting was finally going to move down to second place and sculpture would be third. So I jumped to the computer, which was simply playing with a new medium. I found the deep space of computers exciting, the idea of going in and in and in, like perspective once offered. But there were almost too many possibilities. For young artists, doubt doesn't exist anymore because of computers. Things can be so easily erased. That's why young artists are so confident. They don't think they have to make choices. But in the end, they do."

"You had a show of your computer prints which contained figures. You must have had confidence in them. You sent one to *Vanity Fair* that contained recognizable people, didn't you?"

191

"It's not an asset to try for Beauty. We stopped believing in the capacity of our art to give an emotional jolt as soon as making figures counted against you."

"So you tried for a jolt with *Rape of the Muse?*"

"The art world is very subtle. No critic would ever say they turned against Beauty. No one would ever say, 'Michelangelo's work isn't beautiful.' They would say, 'His work is not ours.' From that viewpoint, they can imply that Beauty doesn't really matter without ever having to say it. Very subtle, isn't it? Your early modernists, your Brancusis, your Picassos, believed in Beauty; they had the same values as their elders. They just needed to express them in present terms. Your Minimalists and your Pop artists weren't interested in any of it."

"Were these concerns at the root of your arguments with Mr. Pruhar?"

"Listen. I'm willing to give Simon the disc of *Rape of the Muse* right off my computer. It's the only copy I own. He can do with it as he pleases."

He denied all wrongdoing and Pontes reinforced his stance. When Montrose rose from the witness chair at the completion of this testimony, his supporters applauded.

cy∂

"She told me a lot about you," the small woman said, stepping up to me as I walked out of the courthouse. "I'm Binny's sister."

Julia looked at me in a friendly, interested way and fussed with her loose tan blouse that had a small string at the neck instead of buttons. She had bitten-down nails and a serious face. It must have been horrible to have her rape made public at the trial, to be reminded of it constantly during the three days of testimony.

"Where's Binny?" I asked. In the weeks after she'd told me it was over between us that January, I'd thought many times about the irony of her break-up call. She accused *me* of two-timing *her*—adoring Montrose to the point where I was willing to hand over a private photograph—while all along she wouldn't consider separating from Dave.

"She's with Timmy," Julia answered. "But she wanted to know if you were still painting."

"Tell her I've had some trouble, but I've been working at it."

"She told me you didn't mind being alone."

"I don't."

"Binny hates being alone."

"So I've learned."

"And she loved being with you."

"And with your Timmy," I said.

"It's good to know she talked with you about him."

"All the time."

"Last year, Binny lived up in Albany with us for three months. It was heaven. Like I had a real family again."

"I probably know Timmy better than I know any other kid, and I've never even met him," I said. "She talked about him plenty."

"I'm glad. I'm glad that she was honest with you." She gave me a quick glance.

Too honest, I wanted to say, but I felt we were having one conversation while another parallel unspoken one was going on. The unsaid one went something like: 'Sometimes Binny is too honest, and that's hard on everyone.'

Binny had described her sister as remote, but I could tell she was a woman who judged no one. Still, I sensed she was uncomfortable.

"You don't know, do you?" Julia asked.

"Know what?"

"That I keep Timmy for them."

"Keep Timmy for who?" Now I was confused.

"For Binny, for Dave. I've had Timmy since he was a baby because Binny didn't want to raise him in the city."

She actually looked defiant, proud, after this remarkable statement. As if there was no time for pettiness or old grievances between sisters. She smoothed her blouse and faintly shook her head.

It took me a moment to understand. Had Binny sent her to tell me this news? Had she somehow judged it was time for me to know that Dave was Timmy's father, and if so, why hadn't she mentioned it herself months ago? Was there more to confess? Binny had resuscitated my painting life, but it saddened me to think I would always wonder what else she hadn't told me. No wonder Julia had taken care of Timmy; Binny must have taken care of her after the rape.

I saw Binny then. She was lower down the courthouse steps holding Timmy aloft, making him laugh. She'd become a perfect stranger again. I was deeply hurt by her lies. I tried to see her with some balance. I went over to her. I studied the two strands of her fake pearl necklace. Her nostrils were small and her lipstick bright. Her earrings hung like silver kite strings.

"Julia told me," I said. I felt bad for Julia. I understood that Binny sent her money, but wouldn't compromise her life. "So this is the famous Timmy." He had wide, almond eyes and a squashed distance between his lips and mono-brow.

She saw me staring at a deep purple bruise on her forearm.

"He bit me again. The only time he gets frustrated is when he's overexcited. It really hurts when he bites.

"She's a better mother than I'd ever be. I thought Timmy would do better with other kids around. I couldn't raise him." She sniffed, fighting tears. Her eyes, which usually had a laughing glow to them, looked miserable. "Even though it took a while, I had to tell you. Dave and I are together. We're trying. After the picture was published, it was the right time to try harder for Timmy."

This information at least revealed her opinion of me—I could absorb every aspect of her life. Maybe certain women are entitled to have things their way. Perhaps she wanted to see me again; naked, she was not a small forfeiture. But I knew if we had continued together I would have paid a heavier price.

∾

At two o'clock, Pontes began the closing arguments.

"I think that we have been here long enough so that I don't need to articulate at great length the facts that were found in this case, except to summarize a few of the more interesting ones. I have actually heard no factual basis for Mr. Pruhar's claim that there should be an award of punitive damages under any circumstances, lest possibly his belief that he wants to punish my client, the defendant. I don't think that's sufficient. In fact, for there to be punitive damages, there must be malicious intent by the defendant. Here, as far as Mr. Pruhar is concerned, the most he shows is a sense of paranoia at the loss of his friends. *Gee, these people still talk to Harris Montrose, but they won't talk to me.* Perhaps Mr. Montrose is a more engaging artist; perhaps these people sympathize with Mr. Montrose for having undergone a lawsuit where there is no evidence of wantonness or maliciousness. Mr. Pruhar wanted to punish my client. There is simply no showing here of a heedless disregard for Mr. Pruhar's rights." He lifted his shoulders, perplexed.

"In fact, if anything, there is a showing that these two artists had a long, somewhat embittered philosophical battle, and that Mr. Pruhar has never liked the depiction of any figures, preferring abstractions. And the defendant expressed in his form of communication, a computer-generated picture, his views on philosophy insofar as it relates to the plaintiff. It's not a lot different than if my client had said to the *Vanity Fair* writer during his interview, 'Mr. Pruhar is turning against art, he's injuring art, and when he injures art, he injures me.'

"The next matter goes to the pleading on compensatory damages. The plaintiff has failed, as a matter of law and as a matter of fact, to prove that this was libel per se. First, it did not disparage him in his profession. Mr. Pruhar continues to work

195

as a professional artist. Indeed his ceramics trade is booming. The facts show that not one person thought he was violent, not one person thought he was a rapist, not one person kept away from him, not one person wouldn't talk to him, not one person 'believed' Mr. Montrose's picture. Mr. Pruhar's friends are artists. They knew the picture wasn't true. He couldn't find one person to come into this court and say, 'For months I kept away from Mr. Pruhar because I was afraid he'd draw a knife on me or rape me.' I cannot then see how one could find that this picture constitutes a libel. Anyone who looks at it knows it is an allegory. Anyone with a reasonable mind knows it's not true. All we have is Mr. Pruhar's paranoia that people weren't inviting him out as much, or talking to him as much. He said he didn't sleep well for one night. This is hardly suffering. This is not libel. But even if it were, libel not believed is not subject to compensation. Thank you."

Barrow stood. "Libel refers to any printed or written statement which falsely or maliciously charges another with the commission of a crime. Obviously, a picture as well as words printed or spoken can be a libel. This picture depicts my client with a knife attacking a young woman, a criminal act. Whether the young woman is half-clad, whether there is a cherub over in the corner, does not give Mr. Montrose the license to portray my client in this way. The sheer fact of showing the commission of the crime, no matter what words you use to describe it, no matter what title Mr. Montrose puts on the picture, presumes malice. If you depict somebody you know, and whom other people know, attacking someone with a knife, it is meant to be malicious. That's libel.

"It's hard to imagine any other view than that Mr. Pruhar was portrayed as committing a violent, felonious act. It is claimed by the defendant that the painting is an allegory, that it symbolizes something other than just a man raping a young woman. The defendant, however, has offered no proof as to what the rapist stands for if he is not a rapist. The only evidence before you is that his mask represents evil with a glimmer of humanity behind it. It's libelous to portray Mr. Pruhar as the personification of evil even with a glimmer of humanity.

"Mr. Montrose did not deny when confronted by people soon after they saw the picture, that he had depicted Mr. Pruhar. Mr. Montrose stated in this courtroom that each person could take whatever view they want of the picture. It is to be interpreted by each viewer in accordance with his own values, beliefs, and lifestyle. To me it shows a man attacking a woman with a knife, and going to the next step, I say if this is representative of a real human being, then it's libel, and then if I take a second step and say that's Simon Pruhar, this picture libels him. The picture does not have Simon Pruhar's name on it. But the jury can, without any extrinsic facts, look at it and see it's him. If it's libel depends only on whether that is my client's face.

"This picture shows Mr. Pruhar as a violent person. I can't imagine what the jurors see in that picture if not that. I submit that if Mr. Montrose had written that Mr. Pruhar is a rapist, is going to be a rapist, wants to be a rapist, was a rapist, attacked a young woman, whatever, no matter how you slice it, if he said that, there would be no question that this would be libel. Here he said it in a picture. By calling it an allegory and sticking a cherub in the corner, he's trying to get away with what he's done, libel, pure and simple."

As Barrow spoke, Montrose didn't look perturbed, his eyes were bright. That morning, when I called to wish him good luck, he told me about the first time a work of fine art had been involved in a libel suit. The precedent was Michelangelo's *Last Judgement* where, legend had it, an Italian cardinal recognized his own face on the devil leading the damned to hell. When he complained to the Pope, the cardinal was told, "If he put you in purgatory, I could have done something about it. But he put you in hell so there is nothing I can do."

"The injury here is to my client's reputation," Barrow said, winding down. "This is the kind of libel in which the law presumes that there is an injury. Although Mr. Pontes wants to sneer about Mr. Pruhar's sleepless nights, I think we are entitled to believe from Mr. Pruhar that he suffered a great deal of emotional upset and an equal degree of injury to his reputation."

When Barrow sat down next to Pruhar, Judge Miller gave final instructions to the jury. "What is libel? Libel is something in print, in writing, or in a picture which defames one's character and is injurious to one's reputation. A libel holds another person up to ridicule, contempt, shame, or disgrace and is a substantial factor in reasonably persuading right-thinking persons to have an evil opinion of one so as to make the injured person an object of reproach, to diminish his respectability and his esteem, change his position in the community or cause him to be dishonored or discredited, shunned or avoided. It is only if you find from the evidence that the picture *The Rape of the Muse* was a substantial factor in having the plaintiff so degraded that you find the defendant committed a wanton act.

"You have now heard the testimony of the plaintiff and defendant regarding the picture, *The Rape of the Muse*. The plaintiff has said that there is a figure in the picture which has a face bearing his likeness. You have inspected the picture here in the courtroom as well as on the light boxes provided in the jury room. You have had the opportunity to observe it closely as well as to observe the plaintiff to determine whether the picture bears his likeness.

"You have heard questions and answers relating to whether or not the picture is an allegory and should be understood as just that and nothing more. An allegory, by dictionary definition, is a symbolical description or representation. It is said to be the description of one thing under the image of another. Most often, an allegory is said to be a story in which people, things and happenings have another meaning, as in a fable or parable. A parable is a short, simple presentation from which a moral lesson may be drawn. Except for the title, we have here a picture in which figures are depicted as substitutes for words.

"Before you reach the question of whether or not the picture is an allegory or an artistic parable, you must first decide whether or not, from the facts of the case and your viewing of the picture and the plaintiff, the face of the figure in the picture resembles or looks like the plaintiff in some recognizable sense. If you so decide, you may then consider whether or not the picture carried with it the impact ascribed by the plaintiff, to disgrace and discredit him in his community.

"There are two kinds of damages being sought here by the plaintiff. The first is called compensatory or general damages which are those compensating the injured one for his injury. If you find the plaintiff is entitled to compensatory damages, then your verdict must be a sum which will fairly compensate the plaintiff for the impairment of reputation; or you may decide even if there was libel here, the injury was so minimal you may make an award which is merely symbolic. The fact that I define damages for you is not to be taken as any suggestion that you are to find in favor of the plaintiff. Your determination must be based on a careful analysis and weighing of the evidence. If you decide that the plaintiff is not entitled to damages, then you need go no further. The verdict will be returned in favor of the defendant.

"The plaintiff also seeks punitive damages. They are awarded to a plaintiff over and above what will merely compensate him, and where the wrong done to him is said to be aggravated, deliberate, intentional, wanton, and malicious. Punitive damages are to punish a defendant for his conduct or to make an example of him. If you find that the plaintiff is falsely portrayed by the defendant as a rapist in the picture *The Rape of the Muse*, then you may award punitive damages to the plaintiff. That is a question you must decide.

"These definitions are given for use only in the event that you find the plaintiff has been damaged. I am not trying to persuade you one way or the other. The plaintiff has asked for both compensatory and punitive damages in the sum of $2 million and $5 million dollars.

"This is a novel case because the plaintiff is alleging that he was the target of libel and his name was nowhere mentioned.

You will have to decide whether or not the face on the figure in *The Rape of the Muse*, is such that the plaintiff has been portrayed in a manner which unmistakably is recognizable to a viewer, or whether some extraneous suggestion is necessary for that purpose. If you do not believe the picture *The Rape of the Muse* depicts the plaintiff, or if you find that in the view of reasonable people the depiction in the picture did not disgrace or discredit the plaintiff, then your verdict must be for the defendant. If you find that it did, then your verdict must be for the plaintiff."

Judge Miller dismissed the jury, announcing to the rest of us his plan to reconvene when the jury had reached its decision.

Chapter 11

Schuyler showed up at my apartment an hour after the closing arguments. I was used to seeing him strike an attitude. In my mind, he was and always would be cocky. Now his neck had welts and his fingers were as thin as scallions. He reminded me of Occo: he gazed at the world as an outsider. Part of me wanted to ask him for a list of all his failures and for an apology about Kittyhake. It would be a form of payment for the gift he'd come for. But I remembered Madeline once saying to me, "You and I are who he has." I'd called her after seeing him at the trial. Her voice trembled and she sounded uncertain on the phone, although she was grateful to hear that he was alive. She had always been his guardian angel.

He didn't want to come inside.

"I'll give you what you need," I said softly. "Montrose's done right by me, so consider this a gift from him."

Schuyler's face relaxed and he smiled. He'd never wanted to become an indigent artist. I didn't ask why the IRS was after him; I didn't really want to know. He had to be a small fry, delinquent for a few bucks, hardly worth the trouble. I wrote him a check, forgiving him and forgiving myself.

❧

I reached the Superior Court building the next morning at nine AM to hear the verdict. The jury had done quick work. On

201

my way inside, I saw that Pruhar was once again doing interviews with the press in the courthouse atrium. He was taking advantage of the final days of publicity. I'd heard that he had had trouble finding investors for his deal with Nieman Marcus. In every *New Haven Register*, *Daily News*, and *New York Times* photograph he was holding one of his prototypes—a pitcher or a vase. It was product placement, a chance to sell his goods and his good looks. He liked standing in front of the atrium's art deco elevator with its beautifully engraved doors that in each interview he compared to his more complex and textured ceramics.

After the assault on day one, Montrose stayed away from the press, but the case was all over the news. Talk of the recently failed Cengal show made him seem vulnerable to TV commentators, and vulnerability was always a positive on television, letting viewers into the "real" Harris Montrose. As one anchorman put it, "He's an artist who's not afraid of sensation."

At Abar Lake, I'd heard his views about celebrity. He thought celebrity provided an antidote for the world's uncertainty. Celebrity provided solid ground; it meant we could all agree on something. The art world—like the movie world, the legal system, the sports world—was always on the lookout for new celebrities, Montrose said. But he believed any celebrity generated by the *Vanity Fair* case would be short-lived and acceptable for the wrong reasons.

I squeezed inside Courtroom 11's door and stood against the rear wall in my usual spot. The rest of the viewers rose when Judge Miller entered.

"Madame Foreman, do you have a verdict?"

"Yes, we do."

"Please tell the court what it is."

"It is for the plaintiff, $100,000 for compensatory and $200,000 for punitive damages."

"Is the verdict unanimous?"

"No."

"Did five of you agree?"

"Yes."

"Thank you for your work. This court is dismissed."

I couldn't catch my breath, but the news stopped no one else. The journalists moved in for their final quotes; half leaned toward Montrose, the others toward the beaming Pruhar. I thought: in a year he will realize what he lost by suing Montrose, a great friend who accepted none of his bullshit.

I got close enough to hear Montrose say, "Winning this suit doesn't let him off the hook, you know." His eyes were narrowed with weariness. He'd expected to win.

"Nieman Marcus or Macy's or Bloomingdale's still may not do a deal with him. *Vanity Fair* will get another article out of the trial, and maybe a third if they appeal the case. I can go back to doing my work."

∽

I drove to Abar Lake later that afternoon. I parked in front of the studio, and looking in the window, was not surprised to see Montrose working at his computer. He stopped every few minutes to go at a hunk of fudge that sat on a small square of waxed paper next to his tools. He shaved off tiny pieces with a plastic knife, balanced them on the end of the knife, and slowly delivered them to the tip of his tongue.

I thought he'd be shaken, his picture renounced as criminal. But I was wrong. He was peaceful after the verdict. He had changed back into his dungarees and white T-shirt. At his desk, gray hair nearly down to his shoulders—hair, he believed, old women coveted for its thickness and wildness—he hunched in his chess pose. Chess, the game of masochism and silent madness. His giant sculptures stood around him high in the air on their pedestals.

When he saw me, he acted like the old Montrose and motioned me in. Before I'd even sat down he started talking about the Renaissance, offering an appreciation of Michelangelo (he called *David* the world's largest homosexual). From

203

Michelangelo he moved to Rothko whom he found gloomy. Then he went back a few centuries in pursuit of the defining attributes of art. "Art was anything that looked like Caravaggio." He bounced to the 1960's when art, as historically understood, came to an end. Since then, art demanded "a philosophical justification and a critical apparatus," Montrose told me. Rubens worked fast but wasn't into elegance, "but then neither were the people paying for his paintings." Art was no longer taught by example or understood through precedent, he said, naming particular artists who had been reviewed in that week's paper. Joseph Cornell was "too clean"; about Malevich, Montrose wondered, "Does anyone actually ever look at his paintings?" He reported that the Louvre no longer had a budget to buy French art that came to market from private collections. France was hemorrhaging important works, he said. The Louvre's director had introduced a proposal for a national lottery to build an acquisitions fund. "Unfortunately, he likes Poussin," Montrose said.

I told him that his speeches during the case had made art into real entertainment again and not just museum-fill. "Quality has taken a big hit here," he said. "I don't know if it even exists except maybe in meats." He told me he'd been approached by CBS to do a television special, but he didn't want to peddle himself. Publicity didn't entice or cheer him. He preferred to stay in the studio where he could again become the unreachable subject of discussion. This was what made Montrose as old-fashioned as much of his figures; he didn't want to be a media star in the age of self-promotion. He also knew that *Pruhar v. Montrose* couldn't compete for long against the next good murder case or Congressman-as-pedophile investigation.

Still, Montrose was famous again, perhaps more so than he had been thirty years earlier. There were now copycats of his work *and* cartoons ridiculing it. He was no longer a recluse, an isolate; he was just a man who'd been away for a while.

Jake and Scout lay on their sides at Montrose's feet, drunkenly pushing around little bags filled with catnip.

"Now *there's* a drug that works. Why can't we get a drug like that for ourselves?" Montrose asked, pointing at the cats. "That's what scientists should be working on instead of the genome. Don't you have some friends who are scientists? Why don't you suggest this line of work to them?"

A packet of Nicorettes lay next to the catnip.

"Why don't you sit in your seat and get to work?"

When I withdrew the bakery box from the shopping bag at my feet and cut the string to open it, he saw the white cake and knew immediately what it meant.

"You shouldn't have," he said, pushing aside his cube of fudge. "Did you bring me a coffee?" We both smiled. "Go get us two knives and two plates." He had me running errands up to the end. "In New Orleans, my father knew this man who ordered every dessert on the menu when he went out to dinner, and took one bite of each."

He understood why I had to leave him, leave New Haven. He saw no point in arguing with me. He knew it was time for me to get back to my art career.

He'd taught me plenty. I remembered the advice he'd once given, and would never give me again now that I was leaving him: you had to think an art audience was crazy if they loved your work, and crazy if they hated it; and it should make no difference either way or you'd be opening yourself up to the opinion of the world.

"Hey, good luck with it all in New York," he said, licking the frosting off his fingers. He'd slipped into the voice he used when he wanted to say something sincere, but didn't want it to seem sincere.

I knew he'd get a new assistant, and he'd never call me, but he'd be glad to talk with me on the phone from time to time when I called him, and would welcome any visit.

My question—Can you make great art in the suburbs?—had been answered. Before I knew Montrose, I would have had to say "No." But he could have lived anywhere and done important work. He just happened to follow Pruhar to Connecticut.

I had to return to New York. My ambition had grown quieter but more available to me. I had a life to live in New York even without Binny. I'd lined up a job at a design firm to employ the computer skills I'd honed at Montrose's. I had been a painter since I was sixteen. But Montrose had taught me the computer was very powerful. He could work for a week on a computer image, and if he had given that image to the slickest Dutch painter of the fifteenth century who every day of his life had practiced capturing light off crystal, that painter couldn't have given back eighty percent of the quality. Computers put a premium on the imagination and not on hand-to-eye coordination.

I didn't tell Montrose that I'd scanned a photo of my Binny painting into my home computer, and I'd scanned in the photo of Binny that Montrose had made famous in *The Rape of the Muse*, and I'd overlapped the two. No art critic was interested in oil paintings any longer. To interest people, I needed to reformulate my work. The point was to make people look. That's where there was hope for the visual arts. Binny in paint and Binny photographed, laid over one another, painted knee over real knee, back and forth, real and painted. Call it ambiguity or transformation; Montrose called it "the flip." It didn't have all the tactile qualities of paint, but Montrose was right: the computer had invented a new space. The artistic question of this millennium was what to put in that space. And it had to be a subject that had never had a space to hold it before, and it had to be Beautiful.